Danny's Song
A Promise Made is a Promise Kept

By Daniel W. Martin

Table of Contents

Chapter One

"I hate traffic," Dan thought as he sat in his Grand Prix with his wife, Kathleen, in a long line of other people who probably hated traffic as much as he does. They, however, have likely adjusted to it as it is an everyday occurrence with them in a city like Cincinnati. Living most of his recent life in a small town in the Midwest, the 5:00 rush hour is two cars at the same 4-way stop.

"We should have started for the ball park an hour earlier," Dan muttered to himself. The ride to the Great American Ball Park that day had started an hour and a half earlier in Danville, Kentucky. He and his wife had made good time on I-75 until they got off the exit for the ball park.

"Dear, it's really not that bad. It's only a little further that we have to go. Most of these people don't have it nearly as well as we do," his wife said, forgetting just how good her hearing was compared to his.

"She was right," Dan thought. All they had to do was make it to the ball park and flash their World Series V.I.P. credentials given to them and the Red Seas would be parted, or so they were told.

"Do we have to listen to the radio that loud?" Dan's aggravation went from the traffic to his wife. "Listening to the radio should not be a struggle," he thought to himself. Rather than fight that fight, he just clicked the

1

radio off. "My, aren't we in a good mood," his wife responded sarcastically.

On his left, another lane of traffic heading in the same direction, only a little faster, wouldn't you know? Eventually, a group of motorcycle riders had eased up beside them. Dan thought that must be the life, hit the open road and ride with the wind, as free as the wind.

Dan looked over at the first rider alongside his car. The rider, probably in his mid-thirties, had on an un-buttoned white baseball jersey with red pin stripes and an old Cincinnati Reds' ball cap, turned around backwards. He looked like a throwback to the '70's era Reds team. Dan didn't realize he was staring as he admired the motorcycle the guy sat on, a Harley style v-twin, custom paint, fat back tire and of course, loud chrome pipes. Suddenly, the rider turned and looked at Dan, catching him by surprise. As if he was reading Dan's mind, he looked Dan straight in the eye, gave him a smile, a thumbs-up, and eased a little further up his lane.

"Probably a nice guy," Dan thought to himself.

One by one the riders passed Dan's car as he had the opportunity to admire all of their bikes, each one of their bikes were like iron stallions that each of the riders commanded to do their bidding. Dan wondered what their lives were like and in doing so, made him feel a little less about his own life.

As the last rider puled slowly by, Dan noticed this one was a handsome young man, probably in his early twenties, with a baseball jersey on and backwards ball cap as well. This young man stood out from the others in one distinct way, perfect, up-right posture. This guy sat tall and proud on his bike and as he pulled past Dan, looked over, smiled and waved, like he was someone Dan knew. On the back of his jersey, Dan saw the name "Stan".

"Someday," he thought to himself, "that's going to be me on a bike like that."

So with the motorcycle riders gone, there he was, sitting in the silence of his own thoughts when . . .

"A promise made is a promise kept."

Slightly startled, even after all of these years, Dan sat up like a child in class who had been unexpectedly called on by his teacher. Without really thinking, he took a quick look in the rearview mirror to see if someone had somehow slipped into the backseat of the car.

"What is it?" his wife asked. She rarely misses a thing and realized that something had happened.

"Nothing," he said and then continued in his silence. His wife, sensing his quietness signaled something else, asked, "Are you hearing that voice again?"

Pausing before responding, not knowing if he should be truthful or just blow it off, Dan responded affirmatively and let it drop. Fortunately this time, she did too. He thought he would have been used to it after all these years. It had always made him feel like a nut case to hear such things, distinctly and crystal clear, that no one else ever heard. It was always the same voice, somehow so familiar, but yet so distant and forgotten.

Finally, the line of traffic made its way up to a gate where they were supposed to turn. The gate, tended by many, many guards, led to a secured entrance into the Great American Ball Park. The guards looked at the car and then at them questioningly, apparently more used to celebrities and other dignitaries arriving for the game in limousines rather than a couple of everyday people in a 14-year old red Grand Prix with over a 185,000 miles on it. Now they would see if the Red Seas would really part or not.

"May I help you?" the guard asked, suspecting that Dan was either lost or trying to weasel his way into somewhere that he was not supposed to be. Dan handed him his World Series V.I.P. credentials. The guard looked at him, looked back at the credentials, and back at him and his wife.

"Do you have your tickets as well?" the guard questioned. Dan reached into the console and handed him the tickets.

"Right beside the Reds' dugout…these are very good seats, probably the best tickets in the house.   Mr. Morgan, if you will drive up to that booth where those two attendants are stationed, they will direct you the rest of the way."

"My, my, my, we are important, aren't we?" his wife replied after they took the credentials and tickets back and were out of earshot.

They drove up to the booth where the two attendants came out to greet them, one on each side of their car, opening the doors for them to exit. Valets . . . not exactly something he was used to. Dan stepped away from the car as the valet jumped in and drove their car further out into the parking lot. The attendant looked at their credentials and took their tickets. He introduced himself as Keith, or Kevin, or something or other as Dan could never remember names so just remembering a first name was an accomplishment, and asked if they would please follow him.

Into the bowels of the Great American Ball Park, through a long tunnel they marched, a left here and a right there. Most other people within the tunnel looked somewhat official and like they belonged there. Dan felt like a fake, like he really shouldn't be there at all. After a lengthy walk, they came out of the tunnel just above the home team Reds' dugout. A few rows down from the tunnel exit, Keith stated that their seats were right there, pointing to two seats right behind the dugout. "If there is anything at all that you need, I'll be glad to get it for you."

"Very impressive seats," Dan said. "At least we aren't in the nosebleed section, with binoculars, surrounded by loud, obnoxious, drunk people that you ordinarily couldn't pay me to be around. I could get used to this."

"You wish you could get used to this," his wife said with a smirk.

And so they settled into their surprisingly comfortable seats. Of course, after years and years of aluminum bleacher butt, it didn't take much in the way of cushioned seats to impress them. They were supposed to be accompanied by Kathleen's brother and his girlfriend, but a last minute business emergency that her brother had to attend to ended up leaving Dan with two extra tickets and a buffer between them and the people in the next seats. Dan didn't mind.

Now the sheer immensity of the stadium was impressed upon them. With all of the people and all the commotion around them, Dan could not help but be a little unnerved. He wondered how similar this was to the coliseum back in Roman times with gladiators warming up and the throngs of people screaming for the Christians to be brought out . . . such a morbid thought.

One hour before game time, Dan's mind began to wander and he began to ponder . . . "I could have been, I should have been, down there on the field."

Chapter Two

Summer of '66, Coach McGuire had selected a 9-year old Danny Morgan who was in his second year of baseball. This was McGuire's first year of coaching and for all practical purposes, Danny's first year of baseball. The prior year's season playing time amounted to no more than one time at bat for which he only managed to foul a ball off before striking out.

However, this year was different. The coach was really a coach and he saw promise in the 9-year old. He needed pitchers and Danny was a skinny kid that seemed to have a gift for throwing. And so Danny threw.

Danny's first game that season was tense to say the least. His parents were in the stands and the park was full of kids he knew. He felt the pressure of potential failure in front of him with his dad sitting in the stands before him. Plus, the kids at that age were merciless when one of their buddies, one of their own, failed. In retrospect, perhaps they wished for another kid's failure to make up for their own. He could sense the prospect of his friends picking on him like vultures picking flesh off of one of nature's hapless victims. Full of nerves, he didn't pitch; he threw, pretty much all over the place, but for his first time out, not too bad.

After the game, the players lined up at the concession stand to get their free after-game drink, well, not exactly free since the parents of the players took turns paying for the player's drinks. A man that Danny didn't recognize at first, a man in dark blue, came up behind him. He looked huge, an older man with light brown hair, cut rather short, sporting a light goatee and wearing a big smile. Then Danny recognized him as the umpire behind the plate in the game they had just played. The umpire was between games and taking a break.

"Danny, come over here. I want to talk to you."

With a lump in his throat, Danny didn't know what to say or how to respond. The umpire wanted to talk to him. Did he do something wrong? Was he in trouble? Why did he want to talk to him? How did he know his name?

Fortunately, the umpire had a smile on his face. Sensing some intimidation, the umpire sat down on the bleachers so as to minimize the difference between his 6'4" frame and that of a skinny 9-year old kid.

"Not bad for your first time out, Danny. You weren't nervous, were you?" he asked, already knowing the answer.

"No, sir," was all Danny could manage to get out, ...and a lie at that. Danny thought the umpire knew it was too as he paused a long time before he spoke again.

"First time's the hardest but it will get easier from here, I promise. I bet your parents are proud of you. I would be, no, that's not exactly right, I am proud of you."

Not knowing what to say and still apprehensive about his first meeting with the umpire, Danny stood in awkward silence.

The umpire seemed un-phased by the silence, …and he continued.

"Danny, do you know what the first 'secret' rule of pitching is?"

Another moment of silence passes and then the umpire said, "Well, I guess 'secret' isn't exactly right either. I sometimes just use that word to get people's attention. Sometimes it seems like most people don't pay that much attention to the obvious unless they think it's 'secret'. But that's not what's important right now. What I was going to say is that the first rule of pitching is not really a secret, and it's actually more than a rule . . . it's a commandment. You have to be able to throw a strike when it's needed. If you can't throw a strike when it's needed, you'll walk every batter and the game is as good as over. Pretty simple, huh?"

"Yes, sir," came a meek reply.

"Do you know what you need to do to learn how to throw strikes?" His question was followed once again by uneasy silence. Danny felt like the teacher at school had called on him to answer an easy question, one that he didn't know, in front of the whole class.

"Practice," said the umpire. "The 1st Commandment of Pitching, is 'Thou Shalt Practice Throwing Strikes.' Pretty simple, and pretty obvious, huh?"

And with that simple advice, Danny's first meeting ended with the person whose name he would never know, but would always think of him and remember him as the Man-in-Blue. From then on, after some encouragement from the coach, Danny's dad would occasionally get out in the backyard and practice catching him.

The season would often find Danny at the Little League ballpark whenever there were games. Danny would be watching the game, positioned on the hill behind the bleachers to get the best jump on any foul balls that made it over the backstop. Foul balls could be turned in at the concession stand for bubblegum and he loved bubblegum, especially free bubblegum that he beat the other kids out of. Each piece was like a prize.

Danny's pitching did get better, and the umpire, the Man-in-Blue, gradually came to be not so intimidating, always with a smile, a word of encouragement, and sometimes a break on a called 3rd strike. He was almost a friend, that is, if he hadn't been the umpire and as big as a tree. By season's end, Danny was the best pitcher on the team. The season ended with Danny pitching a shutout in the league tournament championship game. Danny was a hero, a hero with his first trophy.

Chapter Three

"Where is your mind?" Dan's wife asked as he quickly came back to the "here and now."

"Just trying to take everything in," he replied.

There was some truth to that reply. There was a lot to take in; the immensity of the stadium, the mass of people filling it, the high definition, LED, 218 foot wide scoreboard and video screen showing players' stats, highlights, and the occasional candid-camera shots of people in the stands. The flash of the cameras was a constant from the people in the stands. TV cameras were set up throughout the stadium, everywhere, so that nothing was missed, no angle not covered, for re-play, re-re-play and analysis. On the field some of the players were already being interviewed about the 7th and final game of the World Series.

Dan could see the starting pitchers warming up in their respective bull pens. The Reds were starting a rookie pitcher. With the pitcher was an older gentleman in a Reds uniform. Dan suspected that this was the pitching coach. He could see the man had Clemons on the back of his jersey. Looking in the program, Dan saw he was indeed the pitching coach. At that point there was probably little more that could be taught and you just had to hope the kid remembered everything. The coach had one of those looks on his face - maturity, wisdom, experience, and something else. Dan wasn't sure what it was. . . just a "knowing" kind of look.

Dan put on the earphones of his radio so he could pick up the broadcast. The radio announcer was asking the manager, in such a critical game, whether it was a smart move to start a rookie pitcher in his first major league appearance in the final and deciding game of the World Series. This particular pitcher was the last to be called up from the Triple "A" farm team before rosters were set-in-stone for any post-season play. The manager had been put in a difficult position with season-ending injuries to two of his pitchers in his starting rotation. That, combined with the series going a full 7 games with three of the 6 games played going into extra innings, his pitching staff was stretched to the limit. The manager really had no choice but to start the rookie and hope for the best. The manager told the announcer that the youngster had spent the last three years working his way up to Triple A this year and had been their "go to" guy all the way there. That was the best spin the manager could give as an answer to a tough question that was subtly calling into question his judgment.

Chapter Four

The next year found Danny in Little League as a 10-year old. Tryouts were intimidating. His dad was there as were all of the other parents and kids hoping to make the jump from Minor League to Little League. He need not have worried; his natural ability was developing quickly. Coaches would be quick to grab a young kid with promising talent.

His baseball coach from last year was now a coach in Little League, but unfortunately Danny did not end up on his team. He ended up on another team, the Colonels, who, as luck would have it, had a poor team last year thus excellent draft picks in the tryouts and Danny was it. Danny was further disappointed that the Colonels' coach didn't do so well with the rest of his selections and the team did not look all that good. However, his new coach was a kind old man that took Danny under his wing.

Danny coaxed and badgered his dad to practice his pitching in the backyard with him. His dad probably didn't recognize the importance of baseball to his son. Even if he had, his dad probably would not have known how to help him. Growing up during the Great Depression in a shack situated on a steep hillside overlooking Howard's Creek, his dad never had the opportunity to play organized ball when he was a kid. There had been more important issues to deal with growing up then, like where your next meal was coming from.

Growing up, Danny idolized his father. His dad would tell him of his life down on the Kentucky River, stories of hardship and strife. But to a kid who had hardly been out of his neighborhood in the city, they sounded like Huckleberry Finn adventures.

But hardship and strife became much more real for Danny when he went to visit his grandma and grandpa down on the Kentucky River. They lived in a shack on a steep hillside overlooking the river. His grandpa was not his real grandpa. His real grandpa had been murdered long before Danny was born. Who he called his grandpa was really his great uncle Stan. Stan lived a hard life. He was afflicted with a condition in his back that caused him to be in a perpetually hunched over position since shortly after he got out of the army. He had lived the rest of his life like that. Besides a modest disability check, what little income he had was made selling fish he caught out of the river to whoever would buy them. His boat was an old wooden row boat that got him up and down the river. There was no car. Rides to town had to be asked for to whoever was going in that direction. There was no running water in the shack. Water had to be carried in buckets from a springhouse down the road. His restroom was an outhouse on a path along the hillside. Heat in the winter came from a coal burning stove in the main room. And Stan was not by any means a handsome man. His looks were as ugly and hard as his life had been. But inside, he was beautiful, at least in Danny's eyes.

Now that Danny was in 'Little' League, things did not seem so little to a 10-year old now that he was surrounded by bigger and stronger 11- and 12-year olds. But he could pitch and he could throw strikes and that's what got him playing time.

Much to his delight, the Man-in-Blue was also umpiring again this year. Danny really appreciated the games when he was behind the plate calling balls and strikes. Not only did Danny seem to get some strike calls when he might not have deserved them, but even when he threw a ball clearly out of the strike zone, it just didn't seem very far out just due to the Man-in-Blue's immense size behind the plate. He seemed as big as the backstop and was sometimes just as effective on some of Danny's pitches.

Danny noticed that the Man-in-Blue always seemed to be at the ballpark. He would be umpiring, watching games, or sometimes just talking to some of the kids. He seemed to be interested in all of them. Danny enjoyed the time that the Man-in-Blue would spend talking to him. Not only did it make him feel special, it gave him comfort knowing he was there.

One day at the baseball park, not paying any particular attention to anything, there he was, the Man-in-Blue.

"Becoming a regular pitcher for the Colonels, are you? I've been watching you and I think you'll make a good one, and a better one when I tell you the 2nd 'secret' rule of pitching. OK, so it's not really a secret, but it's more than a rule. It is a Commandment."

Once again, the Man-in-Blue had Danny's attention and he was riveted as he waited for the sacred knowledge of baseball to be bestowed upon him.

The Man-in-Blue continued, "Batters only get three strikes and most of them take the first pitch. A batter usually wants to look at a pitch first to get his timing down and see how hard you can throw. If you throw the first pitch a strike, you only need to throw two more strikes and he only has two chances left to hit the ball instead of three, so the odds are more in your favor. They call it 'getting ahead of the batter.' I call it just being smart. So the second commandment of pitching is 'Thou Shalt Throw a First Pitch Strike.'"

Well, that was all it took. The Man-in-Blue told Danny the 2nd great Commandment that he should know. Plus, he said Danny would be a "good one." Maybe he meant great. Danny wanted to be a pitcher more and more. Nothing happened until the pitcher pitches. The pitcher was in charge and everyone had to wait on him.

Chapter Five

Back at the stadium, batting practice and warm-ups had ended and the teams had secreted themselves back in their locker rooms, no doubt for the pre-game speech designed to motivate the players to put their game face on and play their 'A' game. Dan's mind went to the new kid on the team scheduled to be the starting pitcher for the Reds. His first major league appearance and it's starting the final and deciding game of the World Series. Dan wondered if he felt that he was up to the challenge, or if he felt like he was a Christian being fed to the lions for the amusement of the rabid fans in a Roman Coliseum. For better or worse, this would undoubtedly be a defining moment in his life, more than any other.

Dan thought everyone connected with the teams had left the fields but then he noticed the older gentleman, who he learned was the pitching coach, was still out there in the bull pen talking with another gentleman dressed in dark blue clothing. The clothing reminded him of the umpire's standard game clothing. They were there for some time, and it made Dan wonder . . . . He just had a feeling that it was a very interesting discussion they were having.

Chapter Six

The Cold Creek Little League field was situated in somewhat of a valley in the neighborhood with a creek that ran down the middle of the valley. On the opposite side of the creek were houses whose backyards backed up to the creek. The creek ran through some woods directly behind the ballpark and then on through the neighborhood. Along with the ball field, there were some areas for teams to have practice. The creek was always an attraction to all of the neighborhood boys. Danny was no different. Summer days would often have Danny at the ball park and at the creek, looking for crawdads under rocks, or just throwing rocks at the minnows, or just throwing rocks to be throwing.

It was on one of those occasions that the Man-in-Blue came up behind Danny while he was throwing rocks in the creek. Danny never heard him approach and he didn't know how long he had been there watching him.

But there he was when Danny turned around. By now, there was no fear, no intimidation, just a very big friend, always with a warm smile. The Man-in-Blue was looking through all of the rocks on the creek bank. Danny thought he would pick up a big one like he always did and pitch it into the creek. He could just imagine the Man-in-Blue picking up a huge one and throwing it into the deep water to see a big splash.

Instead of picking up a big rock like Danny thought he would, he picked up a small, flat rock. Danny thought the Man-in-Blue knew he was watching him but he never said a word; he never let on. He took the rock, kinda leaned over and threw the rock like Danny had never seen before. The rock took off from his hand down the creek, sailing low to the water. As the rock lost what little altitude it had, it made contact with the water...once, twice, again and again the rock just flitted across the surface, slowing a little each time it touched the water until the water finally grabbed it and held on with a splash.

"Wow!!!!!" he thought. "What in the world was that? What kind of rock was that? What kind of magic was that?"

The Man-in-Blue didn't say a thing. He just continued to pick up more rocks and throw them just like the first. Danny started looking for rocks like he was throwing...small flat rocks that were easy enough to come by in the creek and he started throwing.

Splash...Splash...Splash....

Something wasn't working here. Danny looked at the Man-in-Blue who was looking at him. He was almost ready to laugh. "Great," Danny thought to himself. Frustration was building with anger right behind it, with embarrassment already having a death grip on his pride. Danny threw another as hard as he could. It only made a bigger splash, as if the water in the creek was mocking his inability.

Danny looked back over at the Man-in-Blue. His smile had disappeared and was replaced by a disapproving look.

"All you have to do is ask," is all that he said.

With that he came over to Danny and got down on one knee. For the first time since Danny had known him, he didn't have to look up to see him. They were eye to eye, closer than they ever had been. Danny was a little afraid. He didn't ever remember him without a smile on his face and a twinkle in his eye. This time he wasn't quite sure just what he saw in those eyes.......something eternal, perhaps infinite.

"This is what you do," he said as he showed Danny how to hold the rock and how to throw it using an entirely different arm motion than the overhand delivery he had.

The first few rocks Danny threw bounced a couple of times on the water before settling down. Not quite as impressive as the Man-in-Blue as his throws would sometimes just skim the water without ever leaving the surface, like a miniature motor boat skimming across the surface.

They spent a good part of that warm summer afternoon skipping rocks, just him and the Man-in-Blue, until finally the Man-in-Blue said it was time for him to go umpire. Danny stayed at the creek a little longer, carefully selecting each rock and practicing his new throwing art until he too left to go watch the ballgame.

The season ended as everyone had expected for the Colonels. They won a few games, they lost a few games…actually more than just a few, but Danny was happy about the season. He was only 10 years old but he had had the opportunity to pitch quite a bit.

Chapter Seven

By now the stands were mostly full. Everyone was everywhere except for Dan's wife, who had gone to the Ladies Room and then on to the concession stand to offer half of their life's savings in exchange for two ballpark hotdogs and Cokes. Dan sat in his seat in the solitude of his thoughts. Gazing up at the scoreboard video screen, Dan focused on the rundown of the evening's starting lineup. The scoreboard would give each player's bio and stats in the same order as the batting rotation. He wasn't familiar with any of them, except for the last of the order, the rookie pitcher, Tanner Morgan....his son.

And then the voice…

"He's the one, Dan; He's the one...My promise to you...through him."

There it was again…that same voice. He knew that voice. He knew he knew that voice. He just couldn't remember…damn it…he just couldn't remember.

And then on the scoreboard screen was his name and his picture, someone had made a mistake. Someone had made a cruel joke. The picture and name were his own...**Dan Morgan - Pitcher**.

Dan's wife was just returning to her seat. She saw the look on his face, staring up into the distance, and knew something was amiss.

"What's going on, dear?"

"Look. Look up there," he blurted out as he turned toward her.

"Where?"

"Up there on the scoreboard."

She turned and looked. "Yes, I see it. Did you ever think you would?" she calmly asked with a huge grin on her face.

"What do you mean?" as he whipped back around to the scoreboard and now saw the picture of **Tanner Morgan - Pitcher**, there where he knew he had just seen his picture and name.

Dan quickly attempted to pull himself back together without being too obvious that he was really quite shaken, and now concerned that the success of his son was apparently having some unwanted and unwelcome side effects.

Still unsettled, he needed to get it together, maybe take a walk around the stadium before the game got going. He quickly said to his wife, "I need to make a restroom trip before the game starts," as a pretext to make a getaway for a few minutes.

And with those words, he was up and working his way up the steps through security and onto the concourse.

"A walk would do me some good, to settle me down and put these thoughts out of my mind," he thought to himself. "If only I wasn't surrounded by a seething mass of humanity. How can I calm down and relax with so much commotion and so many people?"

Dan thought maybe he would have been better off to watch the game at home. But he was there and needed to focus on the game and to watch his son pitch. That was his reason for being there, wasn't it?

Up on the concourse, fans were moving in every direction and it seemed like none of them were moving in his direction...frustrating. The lines to the concessions were a lot longer than he would or could have waited through if he wanted to get back to his seat in time to see the start of the game. Plus, what they wanted for just a hot dog was just criminal. He had not even been to a major league game in years and this trip around the concourse served as a reminder as to why.

Satisfied he was ready to go back to his seat, Dan began to make his way through the crowd. Heading towards the stairs that would take him back down to his seat, Dan saw and heard a commotion that stood out from all of the other stadium noise around him. One section of seats near the stairs was filled with a bunch of loud and obnoxious drunks hooting, hollering, and obviously enjoying themselves, but they were an unwelcome distraction to anyone else around them who wanted to watch and enjoy the game. Those guys all seemed to know each other and had apparently started their partying earlier in the day.

Dan stopped to watch the spectacle. Right in the middle of that mess was what appeared to be a father and son. The boy looked to be maybe 10 or so years old, skinny, wearing a Reds baseball cap, probably a souvenir his dad had bought for him just for this game. He also had a large book of some kind in his lap. The father looked exasperated and frustrated trying to shield his son from the beer being sloshed around and the popcorn being thrown between the drunks.

Normally Dan would have paid scant attention but something inside of him made his feet just stop and stand there longer than he normally would have. He felt for the father. There was not much a guy could do in a situation like that short of just leaving. Undoubtedly their tickets rooted them to those particular seats. It seemed unfair and Dan wished that he could do something, but he knew he wouldn't have much of a chance trying to calm a bunch of rowdy drunks.

But Dan could do something. After all he had those two extra tickets that his brother-in-law and his girlfriend could not use. Dan stepped down to the row that the father and son sat in and finally caught the eye of the father and motioned for him to come over. The father didn't know what Dan wanted and really didn't want to be bothered with another distraction forcing Dan to be more and more insistent. After realizing that

Dan wasn't going to go away, the father finally stood up and made his way past some of the seated loud mouths. "Maybe it was something important," the father thought to himself, since Dan just would not go away.

"Yes, what is it?"

"I can see you're not in the most enjoyable section of seats with…"

"No shit, Sherlock," the father interrupted. "What do you want?"

"Look, I've got a couple of extra tickets to some good seats in the VIP section that my brother-in-law and his girlfriend could not use. Why don't you get your son and follow me?"

The father looked incredulously at Dan, not sure if he was on the up-and-up but when Dan held up the two tickets, it lent him enough credibility with the father that he motioned to his son to come.

"Follow me," Dan said as he hurriedly turned and made his way back to the concourse.

"I really hope I don't regret this," Dan thought.

It was getting closer to game time and Dan wanted a chance to settle back into his seat first. Father and son were right on Dan's heels as he made his way through the crowd and over to the set of stairs behind the Reds' dugout that would take him back down to the VIP section.

They scurried down the steps to the attendant at the beginning of the VIP section, the attendant whose name was Keith, or Kevin, or something, Dan could still not remember. Dan showed the attendant the two extra tickets and told him they were his guests. The attendant examined the tickets, verified their authenticity and allowed all three to continue.

"We're almost there," Dan told them as they arrived at his row.

Moving down the row, Dan had his wife move over to the end of the 4 seats. Dan took a seat, followed by the son carrying that big book and then the father.

The father could not believe his good fortune, not only to get away from that rowdy bunch, but to also get to sit in the VIP section. The father really felt indebted to Dan.

"These are really great seats…"

"No shit, Sherlock," interrupted Dan who offered up a quick smile and chuckle, humorously poking fun at the father's first response to Dan just moments before.

"Well played," said the father, also with a smile on his face.

Introductions were needed now. "By the way, my name is Dan, this is my wife Kathleen."

"Hi, my name is Thomas, and this is James," the father said.

"Dad, my name is Jimmy," corrected his son. Apparently the kid did not like the formalness of "James."

"Hi, Jimmy. Would this be your first World Series?" Dan asked, followed by a long moment of awkward silence. The kid looked like a deer in headlights. He just kept looking at Dan until his dad gave him a nudge and told him to answer him.

"Yes sir, Mr. Morgan, this is my first," the kid finally managed to get out…..and he kept looking at him.

Dan thought, "I didn't say what my last name was. How the heck did that kid know what it was?"

Chapter Eight

One rainy Saturday afternoon that summer, Danny spent the day in the house watching TV. The Cincinnati Reds were playing the Pittsburg Pirates. Danny was a Cincinnati Reds fan. They were the "local" team and the team everyone followed even if they were still about 100 miles from Cincinnati. Danny loved to watch the pitchers; they were the ones in charge and nothing happened unless they started it.

That day Danny saw something he had never seen before. The Reds pitcher was throwing the baseball just like the Man-in-Blue had showed him how to throw rocks to make them skip on the water. Danny learned from the announcers that this guy was named Ted Abernathy.

"Did the Man-in-Blue know this guy? Did the Man-in-Blue teach him how to throw the ball like that? This guy was good.....of course he had to be to make it in the major league," thought Danny.

When the game was over, the rain had stopped and had even dried off somewhat. The season was also over and other things had taken the place in the life of the other neighborhood boys so Danny had no one to throw with. But, being resourceful, Danny had an old tennis ball and an idea. Nearby was his school. The school had a brick gymnasium and on the side of the gymnasium was a paved area. That made for a big brick wall to throw the tennis ball against and have it bounce back. Danny wouldn't need anyone to throw the ball back and off he went.

His old glove in hand and a worn out tennis ball, Danny spent the rest of the afternoon and a lot of others after that, throwing the ball against the wall just like he was Ted Abernathy, not all that different than skipping a rock.

Chapter Nine

The 1st inning of play began and Dan could hear the game plainly through the headphones of his radio. He really appreciated the play by play and color commentary so much more than the rants and ravings of people around him. If it wasn't for Tanner, he would be at home watching the ballgame if he was watching it at all.

Dan's stomach was turning somersaults as Tanner walked to the mound. There was so much noise he could hardly hear his own thoughts. Tanner looked so calm, cool, and collected…like he'd done this a hundred times before.

Tanner took the ball from the catcher and began to show his unusual pitching style, the people in the stands began to take notice. Many fans had never seen this style of pitching. Some were not even aware a person could pitch like that. As Tanner continued to go through his warm-ups, more and more people began to take notice and the stadium began to quiet…still…almost in reverence…and yet 43,000 people in the Great American Ball Park can make a lot of noise even when they are not trying to.

Dan noticed the kid next to him. He was flipping through that monster book he had brought to the game. It looked like it was a collection of baseball cards. Dan had never taken much interest in baseball cards. He had always thought they were only for people who loved baseball but had never played. Dan kept discreetly watching the kid. He was certainly intent on whatever he was doing. Surrounded by 43,000 people, the kid didn't seem to notice at all. Dan noticed the kid finally settled on a certain page. It was as if he found what he was looking for, so he pulled on his father's arm to show him what he found. The father was a little annoyed, but finally turned to look at what Jimmy wanted to show him.

Jimmy pointed to one of the cards in the book and said, "It's him, Dad! It's him! Right there!"

His father looked and looked again. Dan tried not to be obvious that he was being nosey. The father looked up at Dan, and then back down at the book.

"No it's not, it's just a coincidence," his father told him, "now watch the game."

Dan wondered what that was all about. He hoped to get a look at what the kid was looking at in the book because he obviously had some part of what the father-son exchange was about. When the kid turned back around, Dan quickly glanced, but all he could focus on before the book was closed was a page number, 53.

Chapter Ten

One year older and Danny would be one of the regulars on the team, not only as a pitcher but as a player as well. He had been anxiously awaiting the arrival of spring and the start of practice. As soon as the weather was warm enough, he had his old glove and tennis ball out, throwing the ball against the wall, just like skipping a rock. This year he would learn to use that new pitch and emulate the pitcher he saw last summer, Ted Abernathy. Surprisingly it came naturally to him as if he was meant to throw that way. Just as surprising was his Little League coach's lack of objection to his newly adopted style when practice finally started. Being able to throw hard and throw strikes had its advantages.

Danny could hardly wait for the season to begin and to see his friend again, the Man-in-Blue. He had questions for the Man-in-Blue that had been burning his curiosity since last summer.

The season finally began and Danny started the opening game for the Colonels. Just as he had hoped, the Man-in-Blue was there and would be calling the game behind the plate. The game went as Danny had hoped. He threw hard and he threw strikes…and the Colonels won.

After the game and the celebratory free drink, Danny wasn't aware of the Man-in-Blue, but, all of a sudden, there he was standing right next to him with a big smile on his face.

"Nice game, Danny. Where did your new pitch come from?"

Danny explained how last year, after his season had ended, he had seen the pitcher for the Cincinnati Reds, Ted Abernathy, throw that pitch on TV.

"Do you know that guy?" asked Danny.

The Man-in-Blue paused a moment, seeming to look at something far off. Danny even thought his eyes were watering up.

"Yes, I know Teddy. It's been a long time but I try to keep up with how he's doing."

"Did you teach him to throw like that?" Danny asked.

"Yes, in a way I did, it was much like you. I met Teddy while umpiring baseball when he was a kid in a place much like this one, a place that also had a creek nearby. I would spend time in the shade of trees on the creek between ball games. A favorite past time was skipping rocks on the creek, just like you do now. He was an aspiring pitcher and a good kid, just like you. I showed him how to skip rocks, just like you. Next thing I know he started throwing that way in the next ball game he pitched, just like you."

"That pitch put his life on a different path from the one he was on, a different path than the one he would have taken...a path few see, and even less take...a path that leads you away from some things that your life would have led to…and towards other things that you never would have seen. It can be both a curse and a blessing."

Chapter Eleven

Danny became somewhat of a novelty with his unorthodox pitching style. He received more attention than what would have been given to any other 11-year old pitcher. It was that year when he learned the pitch he threw was called a "submarine." Danny continued to follow Cincinnati Reds baseball and especially Ted Abernathy. Bedtimes were often spent falling asleep listening to the Reds on the radio beside his bed.

The Colonels were again a sub-par team, never really in contention for the league championship. It was the Vikings that were loaded with talent, mostly big strong 12-year olds who threw hard and hit hard. They were all very capable of hitting the ball over the fence.

Being the best the Colonels had, Danny got his chance in the fire against the Vikings. The top of their lineup was something to dread for a pitcher, especially their cleanup batter, Rocky Farmer. Rocky was tough and strong and hit home runs, every young pitcher's nightmare. Danny pitched that day like a dream, a nightmare to be exact, from which he could not wake up. Rocky Farmer hit 3 home runs that game and he only batted 4 times. It just didn't seem to matter what Danny threw that day, it was a home run pitch to Rocky. It seemed like no one could help, not even the Man-in-Blue. Needless to say the Colonels did not win.

After the game, the Colonels stood in line for the free, after-game drink. Danny wished so much to have been anywhere else because it wouldn't take long for his vulture-like friends to start picking the flesh off of the crucified young kid. Danny wanted so much to crawl in a hole and make the world go away. He could just imagine what his parents were thinking and feeling right now. Luckily he had ridden his bike to the ballpark and they had driven their car. At least he was spared from the ride home with them. Besides, maybe some accident would befall him on the way home. Maybe he would get blindsided by a runaway truck and he would not feel a thing. It would all be over within the blink of an eye. No one would remember the game. No one would remember the merciless beating and humiliation he had just been subjected to. Everyone would just feel sorry for the kid who was run over by a truck. His whole world had just come to one crashing end, why not another to make it complete?

Danny was just about to make his getaway on his bike for the long and thankfully solitary ride home when the Man-in-Blue hollered at him from over at one of the picnic tables set up for people who eat their game night meals at the ball park. The Man-in-Blue was more often than not one of those people.

Oh how he didn't want to go over there. Oh how he wished he could just leave and be done with it. But he did as he was told and reluctantly walked over to the picnic tables.

"Tough game today, Danny. Don't let it get you down. Sometimes that's just the way things happen.

39

Sometimes that's just the way things are supposed to happen. Life is sometimes like hitchhiking in a high plains hailstorm. You can't run, you can't hide, and you can't make it go away. You can only stand there and take it. You showed a lot of character today, Danny."

"But there is something you need to remember, no matter how dark it gets,
no matter how hard the rain comes down, no matter how close the lightning strikes, sooner or later, it begins to let up, the clouds begin to break up, and the sun begins to shine again. I've been around a long time and it's never failed yet."

"So what I am saying is …don't whine…don't cry…don't quit…just do your best and try your hardest. It rains on everyone from time to time. Today was just your turn."

Though well-intentioned, the Man-in-Blue's words were little consolation for such a young boy who just had his world trashed.

Realizing that, the Man-in-Blue changed his tack.

"Danny, now that I think about it, perhaps you are ready for the 3rd Commandment of Pitching."

"The 3rd Commandment…. the Man-in-Blue was going to tell me the 3rd Commandment of Pitching. Why couldn't he have told me sooner," he thought, "like before this game?"

It seemed like such a disconnect, like the Man-in-Blue was totally unaware of what had just taken place. But the Man-in-Blue nonetheless began to speak.

"Once you have mastered the 1st Commandment of Pitching, to throw a strike when you need to throw a strike, and when you have mastered the 2nd Commandment of Pitching, throw the first pitch a strike and get ahead of the batter, then you are ready for the 3rd Commandment of Pitching. You need to have more than one pitch, something more than a fast, straight ball. If you always throw the fastball, the batter will get used to seeing it and if he sees it enough, he'll start hitting it. That's why you need to keep them off balance, not knowing what to expect. Pitchers do that by throwing different pitches and at different speeds."

"I've never been a pitcher, or a player, but I've watched them for what seems like an eternity and I've learned a thing or two. You know you throw the ball as hard as anyone in the league. A batter has to really be on his toes to get the bat around quick enough to hit the ball. Once in a while, why don't you just pretend that you are going to throw the ball hard but then throw it about half speed and see what happens. I think you might be surprised."

Danny still didn't know what that was going to accomplish. The Man-in-Blue didn't explain, but he paused as if thinking...and then finally, he spoke.

"You are still a little young but I think you may be ready. What you need is a curveball and the way you throw, I think you'll be able to without hurting your arm."

With that he grabbed Danny's baseball and said, "All you need to do is throw a little more side arm, tuck your wrist like this and let the ball come off your fingers like this. But don't forget the 1st Commandment of Pitching, you must be able to throw a strike when you need to throw a strike, and the way to throw strikes is…?"

"Practice," Danny quietly said.

"And the 2nd Commandment of Pitching is…?"

"Get ahead of the batter."

"Correct………….so the 3rd Commandment of Pitching is 'Thou Shalt Mix Up Your Pitches.'"

Although Danny was really given a hard time at school with the ass whooping Rocky Farmer gave him, other games, with a little time and distance, soothed his wounds. The rest of the season wasn't nearly as bad as that one game. Danny picked himself back off the ground, dusted himself off, and got on with the rest of the season. In fact, the season would include a rematch with the Vikings and Rocky Farmer.

All of the kids were watching the Colonels face off with the undefeated Vikings. Everyone still remembered Rocky Farmer's home run derby against Danny and were anticipating more of the same. This time, however, Danny pulled a curveball and a change-up pitch out of his back pocket and struck Rocky out. The look on Rocky's face was priceless and made it all worthwhile. He never said anything, but Danny thought the Man-in-Blue was very pleased, and proud, like when David beat Goliath.

Chapter Twelve

Few 11 year olds ever made the All-Star team but Danny had hope.......and that's what he did...that's all he could do...hope.

It was early July and the season was at an end. The coaches would vote on the All-Star team and it would be posted on the bulletin board at the ball field. Danny rode his bike to the field with anticipation. Some kids were there on the ball field playing pickup games. Some other people were just milling around. When it appeared no one else was around, he made a bee-line to the bulletin board. Seeing the All-Star team list posted, he scanned down through the names, he scanned once then again more slowly. His name was not there. It felt like he had just been kicked in the stomach. He stood there not able to breathe.

"Danny." A voice behind him broke the silence. "Danny."

Suddenly, panic set in as Danny realized he had been seen looking at the list. Now everyone would know that he thought he was good enough to make the team. How could he have been so stupid as to think he could have made it?

"Danny!"

It was the Man-in-Blue. Danny had not seen him when he arrived at the park. Danny had been careful to check the place over before approaching the bulletin board. Nonetheless, there he was, he just appeared out of nowhere. There was no way to escape now. Danny just wanted to leave and go home, but he was caught.

Danny must have been like an open book to the Man-in-Blue; he seemed to read him so well.

"Danny, you've had a good season. You have nothing to be ashamed of and much to be proud of."

Somehow the Man-in-Blue seemed to know why he was there, what he was thinking, what he was feeling.

"But I didn't make the team."

"There will be more games and more seasons than this one for you. I've watched you now for three years and I know next year will be even better."

"The kids that made this All-Star team, well, for some, it will be their last team, their last game, their last season, and their last chance. I think they deserve at least this one last chance."

"What was he talking about," Danny wondered. "Their last game, their last season, their last chance? He's not making any sense and he's not helping any."

"But I should have made it. I can do it. I know I can. And I want to pitch in the big leagues and the World Series when I get older…more than anything."

The Man-in-Blue was quiet as he looked deeply into the little guy's eyes. Danny wondered what he saw. Danny felt as if he was reading his mind, reading his heart, reading his very soul. Finally he says, with all sincerity, "I know you can. I can see you are already on the path that will take you there. And I know you will."

The look on his face then changes. Danny's not sure what he saw…a mixture of concern with sympathy, empathy with resolution, compassion with firmness.

"But Danny, your path will be different. You will walk your path alone. I cannot take it for you, or with you, and the path will take you through the deep of the forest. It only takes a couple of steps off the path to become lost. But if you look to your heart within, and look to the stars in the sky without, you will find your way there. I promise."

That was the last time Danny saw the Man-in-Blue that year.

Chapter Thirteen

Now a 12-year old, Danny was a senior of sorts in Little League. Having gone through a growth spurt, Danny was one of the taller kids, skinny, very skinny, but tall. That extra height gave Danny the ability to generate even more arm speed and for once, bat speed. The first game had Danny as the starting pitcher. He started off with almost a no-hitter, something he really wanted. But a misplayed ball by the shortstop in the last inning was ruled a hit instead of an error. Nevertheless, Danny came away with an impressive shutout performance and even more memorable was the home run he hit, his first. This was not just any ordinary homerun; this one was hit well into the trees beyond the fence. Danny had never seen anyone hit the ball as far as he had.

After the game, Danny saw the Man-in-Blue. The Man-in-Blue never looked happier, or prouder.

Danny looked forward to everyday when he made his trip to the ball park. Whether or not he had a ballgame, he could always hustle after foul balls or home run balls for bubble gum and cokes and after the ballgame, he would visit with the Man-in-Blue having his hot dog and coke dinner from the concession stand. And there were always the pickup games afterward until dark.

So the season continued. Danny was the dominant pitcher and unexpectedly the leagues long ball hitter as well. It was a shame the Colonels did not have the other players needed to have a championship team.

The Colonels finished in the middle of the pack in spite of Danny's pitching and hitting. Danny of course, was a Cold Creek All-Star at last. The Man-in-Blue had been right; this year was a better year.

The All-Stars had practice every day. Most days Danny would see the Man-in-Blue watching from the stands. It would often seem that he was watching Danny specifically. Danny didn't mind, the Man-in-Blue seemed more like a father figure. His own father wasn't there at practice and wouldn't have been much help to him anyway so he was glad of what help he did get.

The first team the All-Stars faced was against the Southland All-Stars. As with any All-Star game, the stands were full of parents and relatives, including his own. Even the Man-in-Blue was there. Danny would have been surprised and disappointed if he hadn't been there. Danny was scheduled to be the starting pitcher.

Except for the first inning, it would have been a real ballgame. The first three batters up for the Cold Creek All-Stars got on base and then their next batter hit a home run, a grand slam. Danny was the next batter and with bases empty, he hit a home run as well for a 5-0 lead. The rest of the game was a pitchers' duel as the Southland All-Star's pitcher settled down and shut down the Cold Creek All-Stars the rest of the game. However, Danny shut out the Southland All-Stars to keep the win.

After the game, the local newspaper interviewed Danny about his game and his submarine pitching. Danny explained that he learned to throw that way from a friend of his, but he didn't say who. He didn't say it was the Man-in-Blue.

Danny looked for the Man-in-Blue after the game. Danny had seen him in the stands during the game. You would have thought that he would be rooting for his team, but he didn't seem to be taking sides...curious. But the Man-in-Blue was nowhere to be found after the game. No matter, it was celebration time with his teammates and folks, basking in the glory and what the future held for him.

The second round of the tournament was a little closer. The Cold Creek All-Stars had to come from behind to win, 4-3. Danny wasn't eligible to pitch but he did get a chance to pinch-hit and got a single in their rally inning. Once again, Danny only saw the Man-in-Blue in the stands.

The next round of play had the All-Stars at a different field of play. Danny was relieved to see the Man-in-Blue had made it to the game since he was eligible to pitch again. This game would be against the Central League All-Stars. Central was made up of some big kids, mostly black, something Danny had not faced before growing up in an all-white neighborhood. They looked rough and intimidating. They should have been more appropriately called the Philistine All-Stars since Danny felt like he was going against Goliath. He quickly learned how intimidating they were as their pitcher was a tall black kid who threw the ball even harder than Danny. The Central League All-Stars jumped out to a quick lead as Danny was not dominating against these kids; Central played on a higher level. Danny threw his best stuff, keeping the ball down. But it didn't seem to matter; Central hit the ball wherever he threw it. By the end of the 3rd inning, the score was 5-1 in favor of Central. He couldn't strike them all out and he couldn't keep them all from hitting the ball. It had been a long time since Danny had felt pressure like this. He wanted so much to pitch and win. He had plans to pitch in the big leagues; the Man-in-Blue had even promised he would pitch in the World Series.

From the mound, Danny saw the Man-in-Blue in the stands with a look of concern, or was it a look of compassion, on his face? After he finally got the 3rd out, Danny saw the Man-in-Blue on the fence by their dugout. Danny stopped at the fence.

"Salvation," Danny hoped. "Could the Man-in-Blue possibly save me? Could he tell me how to beat these guys? Surely, he would know what to do."

"We haven't got much time left together and there is one more thing I want to teach you if you are going to make it to the World Series. You've got one more card in your hand that you can play. These guys are hitters and good ones at that. They are not going to be looking for a walk, and you are not going to throw the ball by them with sheer speed alone. But they are not without a weakness to be exploited."

Danny was all ears.

"These players have seen fastballs, curveballs, change-ups and all thrown low in the strike zone. So, instead of throwing your curveball more sidearm, throw it more underhanded, a curveball that curves up. And throw the ball a little higher. Tell your catcher to give you a high target. The ball will be coming up at them. They are not used to seeing that and they will swing under the ball."

Danny stood there without a word. Already the 3rd out was made and it was time for the Cold Creek All-Stars to take the field.

"Think about it; think about everything I have said. You'll soon have to find your own way, on your own, without me; it will all be in your hands." And with that the Man-in-Blue rejoined the rest of the people in the stands.

Danny went back out on the mound to warm up; thinking of what the Man-in-Blue had told him. He called his catcher out to talk to him. His catcher was a short, skinny kid named D.D. Sullivan, who looked more like a 10-year old than a 12-year old. However, he was fast, quick and never made a mistake. He was also a pitcher during the regular season who had developed a wicked, slow curveball that made him very effective.

They had even faced off on one game when the Colonels won 2-1 thanks to a 2 run home run Danny hit off of D.D. Danny liked D.D. They had mutual respect for each other's abilities.

"I want you to give me a higher target. And be ready, I'm changing my curveball. I want it to curve up. Don't let it get by you."

"A higher target, how high?

"As high as I can get away with and still be in the strike zone."

"OK, as long as you know what you are doing."

Danny didn't have much time to develop a new pitch in the few warm-up pitches allowed and finally the umpire told the catcher to throw the ball down; it was time to play ball.

Danny wasted no time in going to the new pitch. D.D. was hardly in a crouch behind the plate now; it was more of a half crouch in order to put the glove where Danny wanted it. The batter took Danny's first pitch which was high and a ball, just where he wanted to throw it. The batter was one that took the first pitch. Danny came back with the same pitch in the same place. A swing and a miss. Now his underhand curveball but with a lower target. The ball looked like it would be too low but hung in the air like it was immune to gravity, even rising some; strike two as the batter just looked at it. Now Danny delivered another underhanded curveball with a little higher target. The ball looked to come right down the middle of the strike zone but the spin on the ball bit into the air and climbed up higher and higher as it approached the plate. The batter had already committed to a swing by the time the ball got to the plate. "Strike three, you're out," cried the umpire. Danny's confidence grew.

Danny shut down Central the rest of the way but the Cold Creek All-Stars could only muster 3 more runs; too little, too late. Cold Creek was eliminated in their 3rd game by a final score of 5-4.

After the game, a familiar scene played out for anyone who has had a kid on a Little League All-Star team. The players seemed to be shell-shocked. It wasn't supposed to have ended like this. They had worked all of their baseball lives for this moment. Their parents expected them to win, counted on them to win. Victory was supposed to have been theirs. The coaches and parents alike had made them feel invincible, unbeatable, and the kids not knowing any better, innocently believed it all. Reality hit hard that day. The coaches tried to put a positive spin on the game, the tournament and the season, but for many of the kids, their words were empty, their promises broken. For many of the kids, baseball, and for that matter, life itself would never be the same again. Little did Danny realize, he would be one of those kids.

Chapter Fourteen

Danny was changing as he went into his 13th year. He continued to grow into the 13th year of his life, but only in height it seemed, as he was still amazingly skinny. He was also changing into a young man, and all of that which went with it, especially for skinny, gangly kids.

Life was also changing at home. He wasn't sure why. His mother and father seemed to always be at each other's throat, especially on holidays, birthdays, and weekends. Danny looked forward to the end of the holidays or the end of the weekend and the start of work week. There would be at least a truce in the fighting from the workday separation. Maybe it had always been like that, only now he could see it, feel it, and it was wearing on his psyche.

Danny looked forward to trying out for the Babe Ruth League, which was where all of the better players went to play baseball. If you didn't make it there, you played in the less competitive Thoroughbred League.

Danny had no trouble with tryouts in making a team. Danny's first year was a big jump in so many ways from his last year of Little League. The field looked immense. A ball he would hit out of the park in Little League last year seemed to barely make it to the outfield on the regulation-sized field. The 14- and 15-year olds in the League had some significant growth on him. So as with most other 13-year olds; talent wasn't enough their first year, they needed size as well. Most would sit on the bench until their next year.

This year was also his first year without the Man-in-Blue. Danny just assumed he was still umpiring the Little League games. Although there were times when he thought he caught a glimpse of or heard the Man-in-Blue, behind the plate or around the field and his heart would jump, but it always turned out to be someone else. He missed the Man-in-Blue and the peace, encouragement, and hope that came with his presence. Now it was becoming more and more a fading memory.

The season was one of being in limbo, almost a baseball purgatory where all you could do was just be there, sitting and waiting. Waiting to grow bigger and stronger, waiting for guidance, waiting for direction, waiting for an opportunity, waiting to get in the game even for an inning…and wishing for it all to happen now.

Regardless, there was a 13-year old All-Star team and Danny did make the team. The All-Star coach had a son that also pitched, however he wasn't nearly as good as Danny. But the season ended unremarkably, mostly participating in practices and sitting the bench during the one and only game the All-Stars played as the coach used his son as the pitcher.

Chapter Fifteen

The dream of pitching baseball in the big leagues survived that first year in the Babe Ruth League. The next year he was a freshman in high school, but freshmen didn't go to the regular high school; they were at a separate school called junior high, for 7th, 8th and 9th grade students, but that did not dissuade Danny from his dream, and his intent of trying out for the high school varsity team. Tryouts for pitchers and catchers began in January and consisted of meeting at 6:00 AM in the morning at the high school gym for conditioning and throwing. The conditioning, nothing more than stair laps around the gym with timed suicide drills, was just a means of weeding out those less capable and/or without the heart.

His mom supported his effort to make the team. She was up early to wake him and fix his breakfast, 2 over easy eggs, bacon, toast and a glass of milk. She drove him over to the high school in the cold and dark. She was back by 7:30 to pick him up and take him to the junior high school to finish the rest of his day.

Danny was on a mission and endured the morning after morning trials though he wished he had been more conditioned than he was. Danny threw like always, submarine style.

Hopeful to the end, Danny nonetheless was the last one to be cut at the very end. Danny had to settle for another year in the Babe Ruth League.

Chapter Sixteen

A fire was lit under Danny after not making the high school varsity team. He would do whatever it took in the off season to make the team next year. He needed size and strength. He needed to be capable of throwing harder and harder. Muscles had to be where it was at. He got hold of some weights and a bench and started lifting. No one was around to instruct him so he bought some muscle magazines and devised his own workout routine and spent a lot of time in the musty, unfinished basement of his parent's house doing what he thought he needed to do.

Then in the winter, Danny began running a lot to get into shape. He had already learned how brutal the conditioning program would be once try outs for the pitchers began.

Tryouts began as they had the prior year, showing up at the high school gym in the pitch dark, on cold winter mornings. Danny had benefited from another year of experience in Babe Ruth. The weight-lifting had added some strength and hard earned muscle to a still very lean boy. The winter running had better prepared the young man for the countless wind sprints and stair laps around the gym.

Pitcher/catcher tryouts and practice went on for weeks before the final team was selected. One day the baseball coach, Coach Brewer, called Danny aside for a talk. Until then, Danny had had little actual contact with the coach and really had not wanted to. The expression on his face, his behavior, and his demeanor, left Danny uncomfortable. There was just something about the coach that left Danny with a bad feeling. Coach B, as everyone referred to him, suggested that Danny throw overhand. Danny would do whatever it took to make the team and bring him another step closer to his dream. Danny realized that this man made the decisions on who made the team and later on who played in the games. He realized that this man could decide his baseball fate well beyond the here and now. Danny did not realize until many years later just how right he unfortunately was.

Danny acquiesced to Coach B's wishes. The transition back to overhand wasn't hard at all. He had never entirely quit throwing over-hand; he had only quit pitching overhand.

Danny made the team as hoped. It was a very good team with a number of seniors. Pitching was a strong point. The team had a very strong right- and left-handers for starters. Danny fit in well with the team, someone who worked hard, carried his weight and showed a lot of promise. He felt accepted by everyone. All of the ballplayers had nicknames, just part of the closeness of the guys on the team. There was "Big Red" and "Cola Nut" among others. For Danny, it started out as "Popcorn". Danny had the habit of getting a bag of popcorn to munch on before each game. However, it wasn't too long before it changed to "Yogi" and that stuck. Danny didn't know how the name came about; he just looked at it as a sort of a term of camaraderie.

The season went as well as could be expected for an underclassman at a large high school with a very good, state-ranked baseball team loaded with talented upper classmen. Danny did get his chance to pitch some. One game he even threw a shutout against Estill County. The local radio station in Estill County had even brought their equipment and an announcer to broadcast the game. That was kind of exciting even if he never heard anything they said; just the thrill of knowing that they were talking about him on the radio and that there were people out there, somewhere, listening, was enough.

Danny spent his last year in Babe Ruth League throwing overhand. Whether the beginning of the end began with his change of pitching style (back to overhand) or whether it began with his attitude during his last year of playing in the Babe Ruth League, or both, was really all academic in the end. Danny was a senior of sorts in the Babe Ruth League, and having just come from playing high school baseball, he began to develop a cocky attitude. He felt that he was well beyond almost all of the talent of the League. As the season began, he felt that he should be able to just throw the ball right by everyone. Pitching became a matter of simply overpowering these lesser players. It didn't help his over-confident attitude when he went 5 for 5 in an early game where he hit two home runs. Yes, he felt as if he were a man playing among boys.

Unfortunately, not everyone succumbed to Danny's pitching prowess. Danny couldn't strike out every batter, though he believed he should. That drove him to try to throw harder and harder. That, combined with a happy-go-lucky coach who knew little baseball and less about pitching contributed to Danny's slide that year. Although he made the All-Star team, neither he nor the team went anywhere as they were quickly eliminated in the tournament. The Man-in-Blue and the rules of pitching became fainter and fainter and eventually forgotten.

High school tryouts and practice began as usual in the middle of the winter with early morning workouts before school. It was a given that he would be on the team and would play a more important role on the team since the team had lost its core of talented seniors to graduation.

Chapter Seventeen

If there was one point in time when the die was cast and destiny set in stone, it was early in the season of his junior year on a road game, playing a now forgotten high school team. There was something in the air that night, a kind of excitement or electricity.....or something. It was a very warm evening for that early in the season, the kind of warmth that is temporary and fleeting and quickly replaced by bitter cold, windy wet weather. Danny's team had a comfortable lead going into the late innings. Everyone was feeling good, maybe even cocky. The coach made a pitching change and put Danny in for relief. Danny was caught up in the excitement; he was pumped and his pitching quickly showed it. In his first inning, his fast ball was good, but his curveball was incredible, untouchable. He felt no one could touch him, and they couldn't. The feeling of invincibility fed on itself and he threw his untouchable curveball more and more.....and harder and harder. And then a couple of innings later, there was a pop and some pain in his shoulder. Danny was clueless as to what it may have meant since he had never experienced arm or shoulder problems beyond some minor soreness for throwing too long. So he kept throwing...hard. But the wheels had come off the wagon and the ball never saw the strike zone again. Danny ignored the pain and kept throwing, he was sure it would be alright. But the damage was done, and Danny could not throw the ball over the plate. Batter after batter came up to the plate and quickly had a pass to first base. Again and again and again...the comfortable lead was not so comfortable any longer. The coach, at first in disbelief, was now beside himself. Finally, and mercifully for Danny, another pitcher was brought in to salvage the lead and the game.

The weather had suddenly changed; the wind was now blowing against the team. Whatever had happened to Danny, somehow, mysteriously, seemed to carry over to the next relief pitcher, a tall, lanky left hander. The game was shortly over as the home team only needed to get one run ahead since it was the last inning. The home team was ecstatic, our team…humiliated.

And that was that…until the next day at practice. The warm, pleasant weather of the prior day was replaced by bitter cold, wet weather, but that didn't stop practice and that didn't stop the coach from his retribution at the prior evening's embarrassment. Danny and the lanky left-hander were singled out to throw and throw and throw, in a bitterly cold, windy rain.

It was only at that point that Danny realized how much his shoulder hurt. Danny had had minor muscle soreness before though it always went away; surely this would go away as well, but this time it was different.

Danny saw little opportunity the rest of the high school season, which perhaps was for the best. His shoulder hurt so, so much just to warm up. He found that if he pushed hard enough through the pain, he could reach a point where the pain let up and he could almost throw normally but there was always a price to pay afterward.

He never told anyone of his pain. Complaining was a sign of weakness. Danny felt that the pain would go away eventually as it always had in the past, and to call attention to it may knock him out of any opportunities to pitch.

The only clue that was ever given that something was not right, if anyone had been paying attention, was in his English class one day. He had forgotten an assignment, something about writing a poem about something. Class was just about ready to start when he put the pencil to paper and just started to write what was on his mind.

> The coach was really madder than shit
> And I'm the one he wanted to hit.
> I guess it really was my fault
> That every batter that came up was walked.
> It wasn't that I was weak or soft
> Have pity on me.
> My shoulder fell off.

Danny even drew a little stickman wearing a ball cap with angry stars emanating from his shoulder. Amazingly, the teacher thought it was great and because of her, it ended up in a school publication. The coach was not happy.

Opportunity did not knock and neither did his chance to play that summer on the next level of baseball after Babe Ruth League, a Connie Mack team. That was where he had his sights set. The Connie Mack league consisted of two local traveling teams made up of the better high school players in town. That was where most of his baseball friends went after the high school season. But that didn't happen for Danny. That was the first summer without baseball; it ended up being a lonely, empty summer.

Chapter Eighteen

His senior year on the high school team, Danny knew the routine well, early morning practices for weeks for the pitchers and catchers. His shoulder was still an issue...it still hurt, but he continued to keep it to himself. Coach Brewer seemed to single him out as not giving 100%. Danny realized he needed to step it up on the running stair laps and suicide drills. Although an excellent sprinter, Danny was never a distance person, so instead of finishing the grueling conditioning drills in the middle of the pack, he pushed himself to finish in front.

Perhaps Danny should have seen it coming; others probably did, although no one said a word. One day after practice, Coach Brewer called Danny into his office. Thinking back, Danny can't remember the words the coach used, but no matter how he may have tried to soften the blow, the cutting words shattered Danny's world. Danny was cut from the team. The look on his face coming out of the coach's office was all anyone needed to see. It clearly told what had happened. Danny quickly made his way out of the locker room.

Danny was old enough to drive and usually drove some of the underclassmen on the team home after practice. It was difficult to keep it together in the car; his teammates could see something was up. He could barely get the words out that he was cut.

The rest of his senior year in school was empty. He felt like an outcast. So much of his identity was in being a baseball pitcher and being part of the team. He avoided his former teammates. He felt embarrassed and almost ashamed. He never felt so lonely or abandoned and no one around him had a clue as to what was going on inside this young man.

That year, there was no baseball. That was the year without a summer.

Chapter Nineteen

Danny was now 18, out of high school, and through his first year in college. It had been a long time since he had thrown a baseball and as such, he had forgotten his shoulder and the problems with it. The downtime with his shoulder had been good for him. With that time off, his shoulder had finally healed and that summer another baseball league was formed, this one for 16-18 year olds. Danny learned of this league. Still being 18 years old, Danny signed up and was selected for a team, the Wildcats.

For some reason, Danny started throwing the submarine pitches again in practice. It felt good…it stirred memories of a happier time in his life, and better still, the pain was gone. His coach was a middle-aged man who took a lot of interest in the kids. His coach was not exactly blessed with athletic talent but he had a competitive spirit within him. He took a genuine interest in Danny. Danny needed that. He recognized the unique pitching talent Danny displayed and used it.

It was the first game of the season, first time on the mound in a very long time. It felt so right, so familiar. It seemed like he had just awakened from a bad dream and found himself safe and secure in his own bed, in his own home.

The game went well. The Wildcats won easily. Danny threw very well. His ball was moving good and few batters ever got a good piece of the ball. The umpire even seemed to give him an occasional break on a call when he needed it.

After the game and some minor celebration, Danny was getting a hotdog and coke; he saw the umpire was doing the same.

"Nice game, Danny," remarked the umpire.

Danny was a little caught off guard.

"Thanks," Danny responded.

"I haven't seen anyone throw like that in a long time. Have you always thrown like that?" the umpire inquired.

"I used to throw like that when I was a kid back in Little League. A man who umpired our games showed me how to throw like that, but later my high school coach wanted me to throw overhand."

"And so you changed," the umpire finished.

It was like the umpire already knew the answer when he asked the question.

"You pitched very well. By the way, my name is Jesse. I look forward to seeing you pitch more this summer." And with that, the umpire walked to the picnic tables nearby to eat what was likely his dinner.

Danny occasionally glanced over at the umpire. The conversation brought to mind faded memories of Little League, and of the Man-in-Blue, someone whose name he never learned. This man reminded Danny a little bit of him, but it couldn't have been the same man, even if he did seem distantly familiar somehow.

Each time Danny happened to glance over at the umpire, he seemed to be watching him, observing him.

It was when Danny decided it was time to go, as he was walking to his car when he first heard it…a voice.

"A promise made is a promise kept….if you will only stay the course…and keep to your path."

Danny wheeled around to see…no one. Who could have said that? He looked and looked but there was no one near, no one at all, except for the umpire some distance away still eating his hot dogs.

Danny thought he must have imagined it and went on his way.

That was the first time he heard that voice, a voice that would follow him on occasion in the years to come.

Danny had a great year pitching. His submarine pitch was something that seemed to fascinate people at the park. They would stop to watch when ordinarily they would have moved on with their day.

The games Danny pitched always seemed to have the same umpire as he had the first game of the season. He became a somewhat familiar figure to him, though it was never the same as in Little League with the Man-in-Blue. This umpire seemed more distant, more reluctant…or maybe that was Danny, not the umpire.

The voice Danny heard after the first game of the season would return, usually after he finished pitching a game. Strange and unnerving as it was at first, Danny became a little more accustomed to it, though he never spoke of it to anyone.

The season went very well and at the end of the season there was a bonus. The coaches came up with an All-Star team and Danny was selected. The league was newly formed and there were not many leagues around in the state. In fact Danny had wondered if theirs was the first in Kentucky and being such, they were state champions by default. The coaches lined up the only games they would end up playing, that being a double header with the Indiana League State champions.

A long ride in a school bus someone had arranged on a late summer Saturday took them to their destination. The whole trip was a big adventure, a traveling baseball team, just like the major leagues, even if it was in an old school bus. Everyone on the bus felt the same, excitement was in the air.

Danny pitched the first game and he was "on." Every pitch worked as he wanted it to. Danny's submarine pitch was certainly a novelty to the Indiana team and Danny took advantage of it by shutting them out. The second game went almost as well as they swept the double header. The bus ride back was filled with pride and accomplishment. They all basked in the glory of our a successful trip.

Once back in Danville, he was off the bus saying his goodbyes to the coaches and teammates when he realized he had just pitched his final game of baseball. There was no other place to play...at least not for him.

It was as he was walking back to his car for the ride home when he heard...the voice.

"Danny.........Danny, remember what I have said.............a promise made is a promise kept...........I keep promises.......You keep to your Path."

Again, he was alone...alone in the silence and wonder of the voice. What did it mean?

Danny never played baseball after that summer season. There was nowhere to go...nowhere to play for Danny. No longer did he have any dreams, or more accurately, any illusions of playing baseball in the major leagues. He had pretty much faced that reality and he moved on with his life. His former baseball coach talked him into playing softball for him on another team that he managed and for years that was as close to baseball as he would ever be.

And with baseball, went the voice...for many years the voice was silent...becoming a distant and then forgotten memory.

Chapter Twenty

October 22, 1990, a calm, pleasant evening in a quiet neighborhood in Danville, Kentucky when…"It's time, Dan. We've got to go!" Dan's wife said, calmly, but with a sense of urgency in her voice. The clock had ticked off 9 months. The planning and preparations were about to be put to good use now as they gathered up the necessities of what they would need for the next couple of days.

A few hours later, he was standing in a delivery room.

"Mr. Morgan, would you like to hold him?" the delivery room nurse was asking as she approached him, holding his newborn son in her arms, no more than a few minutes old. Without saying a word, Dan took the bundle she held out to him in his arms as he was overwhelmed with emotion, tears streaming down his face, and he had no idea why.

"A promise made is a promise kept.........He's the one, Danny, He's the one who can take you further down the path to where you want to go.........if you believe."

The voice…Dan heard the words as he had heard them before, never knowing from where they came, but he was so overcome with emotion, his mind was reeling, this time he didn't bother to try to find their source; he was focused on his newborn son.

Chapter Twenty-one

Several years later and several hundred miles away, little Tanner had taken to baseball just like his father had so long ago. Starting off in Tee-Ball, then Little League, Tanner loved to play. He had watched his dad play softball and that was almost like baseball....almost. His dad loved and lived to see him play.

Dan had often practiced with Tanner one-on-one, throwing, catching fly balls and grounders, and batting. For batting, Dan would throw whiffle balls for Tanner to hit. Dan had collected a lot of whiffle balls just for that. You could throw them hard and hit them hard and they did not travel very far or hurt you if they hit you. That way he could throw hard to Tanner without needing a catcher or fielder to chase them.

During the start of Tanner's first year in Little League, a baseball clinic was given prior to the start of the season by some of the local coaches and others involved in the local baseball program. Of course Dan wanted Tanner to go and Tanner wanted to go as well.

There were kids galore that Saturday afternoon at the ball field. The clinic was for kids starting Tee-Ball up through Little League. Dan watched from the stands or along the fence. The kids were broken up into age groups and rotated from station to station where they were instructed in the basic fundamentals of catching fly balls, pop-ups, ground balls, batting, and base running.

It was a long afternoon, but Dan enjoyed watching Tanner; he always made him proud.

At the end of the clinic, Dan's eyes followed Tanner as he finished up his last station. He and the rest of the boys were gathered around home plate where the coaches finished up the clinic with some final comments. This was probably as much for the parents as for the kids as all the parents were sitting in the stands by then to pick up their kids.

Expecting to find Tanner wore out from a long afternoon, Dan thought he still seemed pretty excited.

"You looked pretty good out there."

"Thanks."

Just then it dawned on Dan that he never saw any of the instruction stations going through the fundamentals of pitching. That was the one thing that Tanner was most interested in…learning how to pitch.

"Sorry that they didn't get around to going over the pitching, I thought they would have set aside some time for that."

"That's OK. One of the instructors told me that you would be the best one to teach me to pitch anyway. Dad, can you teach me to pitch?"

Dan was taken a little off guard, and was curious. No one there knew anything about Dan's history with baseball much less pitching. That had all been in a long ago, distant time and place.

"Who was it that said I would be the best one to teach you how to pitch?"

"I don't know who he was; he never said. He was with our group through every station. He was a real big guy, dressed in blue. He looked like an umpire."

Dan had been there the whole time and could not recall anyone like Tanner described. His attention had been with Tanner's group the whole time and a big man in blue did not register.

"Big man in blue," Dan thought to himself.

"Yeah Tanner, I will teach you to pitch, I promise! Tomorrow, we'll start with the first rule, the 1st commandment of pitching."

And they walked to the parking lot to get in their car for the drive home.

As they were leaving the parking lot with all of the other parents and kids…

"A promise made is a promise kept.......You keep yours.......I'll keep mine."

That voice…Dan whipped around and looked, but there was no one around. It was just Tanner and Dan in the car and Tanner apparently had not heard it. But across the parking lot, on the ball field, Dan may have seen a large man…in blue, not unlike an umpire, standing on the bare dirt infield. But it could not have been him.

Dan was quiet, the ride home was quiet, except for the radio, a song by Depeche Mode playing in the background…

"If you need a friend
Don't look to a stranger
You know in the end
I'll always be there."

"And when you're in doubt
And when you're in danger
Take a look all around
And I'll be there."

The voice stirred memories long forgotten. It was, or at least seemed to be, the same voice from another life in another time, so long ago.

From the deepest recesses of a long forgotten past, memories he had been forced to bury and walk away from were now being dug up to haunt him again. Memories of broken dreams he wanted to leave buried and forgotten. He knew those dreams were long dead and could not be brought back to life, and he didn't want to have to deal with them again. The first time was more than enough.

Chapter Twenty-two

Tanner's career in Little League was something that would make any father proud. He taught his little man all of the commandments of pitching that he had learned. They were like seeds planted in fertile ground. All of them took root and flourished in the talent and ability of this little big man.

One day in the middle of the season, Dan was running late from work and drove straight to the ballpark to see his son's game. His wife had already taken Tanner to the field. Dan pulled into the parking lot and hustled over to the stands where he found his wife and took a seat on the hard aluminum bleachers behind home plate.

He saw his son's team warming up on the side lines along 3rd base. Tanner and a couple of other kids were gathered around a rather large man, dressed in blue, who Dan had not seen before and did not recognize. He was throwing the ball to their catcher in the bull pen. He was throwing submarines. The kids gathered around and were all intrigued by his throwing style. Dan watched with keen interest...and remembered. There was a familiarity with this man, but Dan had not seen him at the ball park before. It had been ages since he had seen anyone throw that way and it had been ages since he himself had thrown that way. As Dan watched, the man throwing the submarines seemed to recognize that Dan was there; he seemed to be watching the watcher.

It wasn't long before the game was to start and the coach called for the kids to come to the dugout to hear the lineup and batting order. Dan's attention followed Tanner to the dugout. He knew Tanner would be playing shortstop and batting 3rd. His fielding and hitting had solidified his position when he was not pitching. Shortly after the lineup was called out, Tanner's team took to the field. Dan turned to the bullpen where he had seen that man throwing submarines just moments ago...but the stranger was no longer there. Dan gazed around the ballpark and even got up from the stands and walked around the 4-field complex. He could not find that man anywhere.

The game went as they all had hoped and thought that it would; Tanner's team won 6-4. Tanner had played well, as always.

The team was up-beat about the win, and almost as excited to get their free post-game drink from the snack bar. After Tanner had gotten his drink, he met his parents near the stands. Dan's curiosity was still gnawing at him about the stranger throwing submarines in the bullpen before the game.

"Tanner, who was that guy throwing underhanded in the bullpen before the game?"

"Oh, him...I don't know his name. He always seems to be here helping out around the park. He was the guy at the baseball clinic who said you could teach me to pitch. I thought you knew him. He said you used to throw submarines a long time ago. He said you were one of the best he had ever seen. Dad, do you know how to throw like that? Can you teach me?"

Dan was mystified. He was not expecting the reply he received from his son. Who was that guy? How could he know anything about him?

"Sure Tanner, I used to know how to throw like that. Maybe I still can. Throwing like that is a lot like skipping rocks across the water. Why don't we go to the farm this weekend? You know there are a lot of rocks around that old pond and that's where we'll start."

"He's the one, Dan.........He's the one.......The dreamer must awaken."

The voice again....

Chapter Twenty-Three

Dan's thoughts were abruptly brought back to the stadium. "Popcorn! Popcorn! Get your hot popcorn right here! Only $3! Do I have any takers?"

"This is really something" the announcer said. "Something I don't believe has ever occurred in World Series history; a rookie pitcher starting his very first game in the majors and it is in the final and deciding game of the World Series."

"I think you're right on that one, Marty. I can't imagine what must be going through the mind of that young man being put into this kind of situation. He certainly seems to be handling it all very well, but he has yet to face his first batter. We'll see what happens when he faces the toughest lineup in the American League and certainly the toughest of his career," responded another announcer.

Down on the field, Tanner gives the catcher the sign to throw the ball down to second base. The start of the game is virtually at hand. The catcher takes Tanner's pitch and fires a strike to the second baseman covering the bag and taking the throw. As the ball is being tossed around the infield, the catcher jogs to the mound. The catcher has been in the "Bigs" for several years although this Series is his first. It's been a long Series for him as he has caught every game without a break, even the extra-inning games.

"Tanner, you ready to go?" questioned the catcher.

"Yeah, I think so."

"Did your folks make it here?"

"Yeah, they made it. I saw them sitting just over there near the dugout."

"Good, I'm glad they made it. Just pretend it's 15-years ago and you're throwing to your dad back home. Keep the ball down and throw strikes Tanner, and you'll do fine."

Chapter Twenty-Four

Suddenly Tanner is back in Carthage, Missouri. He's 9-years old and he wants to be a pitcher. He has just gotten through pitching his first game. Patience and perseverance has gotten little Tanner his first chance to pitch in a game. It was hardly a stellar performance. Although little Tanner could throw hard for a young kid, as with most kids his age, he struggled with control. Tanner, being almost a perfectionist who sets the bar higher than a kid should, is bummed out. His dad could clearly see it and steps in.

"Not bad for your first time out Tanner. You weren't nervous were you?" asked his dad already knowing the answer.

"No…well, maybe just a little."

"First time's the hardest, it will get easier from here, I promise. I am very proud of you."

They both stood there, uneasy in their silence.

"Tanner, do you know what the first commandment of pitching is?"

Another moment of silence passes and then his dad says, "The first commandment of pitching is not a secret, but it will be if you ever forget it. You have to be able to throw a strike when you need to. If you can't throw a strike when you need to, you'll walk every batter and the game is as good as over. Pretty simple, huh?"

"Yeah," came a meek reply.

"And do you know what you need to do in order to learn how to throw strikes?" This was followed once again by an uneasy silence. Tanner felt like a teacher at school had called on him to answer an easy question that he didn't know in front of the whole class.

"Practice," his dad says. "Pretty simple, and that's what we're going to do, keep it simple."

Beginning the next day, and from then on, every chance they had, Tanner could be found in the backyard or at the practice field with his dad, squatted down in a catcher's stance catching and throwing back every pitch.

Chapter Twenty-five

It's the end of the Yankees' first time at bat when the announcer said, "And that ends the top half of the first inning. Tanner Morgan hardly had a chance to break a sweat as he threw a total of only 8 pitches and 7 were strikes."

"Well, that's what every young pitcher must learn to be successful in this game. You've got to be able to throw strikes and it's apparently a lesson that this young kid has learned well," replied the other announcer.

From the announcer's booth at the end of the 2nd inning of play, the announcer comments, "Well, after two complete innings, we've still got a scoreless ballgame. Not to say there wasn't some excitement. The Yankees tried to take advantage of an early walk against Morgan but even with three hard-hit balls, the Reds made some of the best defensive plays we've seen in this series."

"I believe you're right on that one, Marty. If the Reds could have only hit as well as they fielded, this game would not be scoreless."

The Reds' 3rd time to bat is at hand and the announcer calls off the players to go to the plate, "Bottom of the 3rd inning and the Reds will lead off with the pitcher, Tanner Morgan. This is a day of firsts for Tanner...his first major league game, his first major league pitching start, his first world series and now his first major league at-bat."

Tanner stood near the on-deck circle easily swinging the bat as he intently watched the opposing pitcher. He had not had a lot of batting practice since being brought up from the Reds' Triple-A farm team, and although it didn't show on the outside, he was very aware of the 42,000 plus people in the stadium who would be watching him.

The umpire was coming back onto the field after getting a much needed cool drink of water on an unusually hot October day. His path back to home plate took him right by Tanner.

"Well Tanner. Are you ready?" inquired the umpire.

"I guess I'll have to be," replied Tanner.

"I see your dad over there near your dugout. I was counting on him being here today."

Tanner was surprised. It sounded like the umpire actually knew his dad.

"Do you know my dad?"

"Yes, actually I do know him, though it's been a very long time. I don't know if he would still remember me."

Tanner was amazed at what a small world this must be. His dad had never mentioned knowing a major league umpire. Tanner was quite intrigued and was about to ask more about how they knew each other when the umpire quickly turned and shouted out to the field, "OK, boys! Bring it on down. We've got a ball game to play and a World Series to decide!!!!"

With that went Tanner's chance to find out more. Tanner was going to have to ask his dad about that.

It's now the 4th inning and the veteran catcher is out at the mound after the last batter struck out.

"Good job, Tanner. Top of the lineup. This guy has already seen you one time. Good chance he'll be zeroing in on your pitches. Get ahead of him quick and then we can work him."

Chapter Twenty-six

Tanner was 10 years old and much improved over last year; all of the practice time with his dad paid off. His strike-to-ball ratio was good. That particular evening, Tanner was pitching against the best team in the league. Tanner had just come back in from pitching another inning. He had thrown a lot of pitches as the other team had a good eye for what was in or out of the strike zone and were not easily fooled. The game was close. Every inning had the potential for the other team to explode with a boatload of runs. Tanner was in need of some help.

His dad, who had been quietly sitting in the bleachers, got up and made his way to the side of the dugout. Tanner saw his dad and knew he wanted to speak with him.

"Tanner, how's your arm doing? Is it bothering you?"

"No, it's fine."

"Are you getting tired?"

"No, well maybe a little."

"You've thrown a lot of pitches. Let me tell you something that may help. It's the second commandment of pitching and that is to throw a strike on the first pitch to the batter. Batters only get three strikes and most of them take the first pitch, especially this team, they are taking every first pitch. A good batter usually wants to look at a pitch first to get his timing down. If you throw a strike on the first pitch, you only need to throw two more strikes and he only has two chances left to hit it instead of three; the odds are more in your favor. They call it 'getting ahead of the batter.'"

So, your first pitch to the batter is right down the middle. OK?"

"OK," replied Tanner, silently kicking himself for not realizing that already.

"You should have figured that out for yourself," he thought.

Chapter Twenty-seven

"Rocky Farmer, hitting .340 for the season will try his hand again at the submariner. Farmer lead the league in hitting on and off during the regular season. Farmer's first time up saw him hit a drive to deep left field but a fantastic effort by the left fielder Hormez pulled it in to save what would have easily been a stand-up double," Dan heard the announcer say.

That name, Rocky Farmer, Dan remembered that name. His nemesis in Little League had had the same name.

"Morgan looks like he's ready. He shakes off the catcher's first sign. Here's the first pitch to Farmer.................Strike...........and the count is 0-1."

Now in the 5th inning and the announcers are commenting, "It looks like the Yankees are finally zeroing in on Morgan's submarines. Joe Tilton started off with a hard single down the left field line. Fortunately for the Reds, Hormez got to the ball quickly and held Tilton's double to a single. Then Jones made a long drive to deep center. Frankly, I thought the ball was uncatchable, but Smith ran a long way and made a fantastic catch at the warning track. Fortunately for the Reds, Tilton thought it was uncatchable as well and was on his way to third when Smith pulled it in. He had to hustle to make it back to first in time. Jones then hit that hard shot between third and short. Now with one out, we've got runners on first and third and......"

The Reds' manager Barkley was concerned. He felt like he was backed into a corner. His pitching staff was depleted and here he was relying on a kid fresh up from the minors. The front office was not at all happy with bringing Morgan up. They believed he needed more seasoning in the minors. They had wanted to trade for someone with more experience to give them added depth to their pitching staff in their run for the Series. But the pitching coach Clemons had been so adamant about bringing up Tanner, he kept telling them, "He's the one," like this kid is going to lead them to the promised land...yeah, right. Who would have guessed they would have ever had to go this deep into their pitching staff.

"Coach Clemons, what are you going to do?!?!?! The wheels are starting to come off the wagon. Get your ass out there!" yelled Barkley.

"...and here comes the pitching coach out to the mound," the announcer proclaims.

"Coach Clemons, the pitching coach for the Reds had been with the Reds' organization for his entire baseball career. Coach Clemons began his career in the Reds' farm club system as a pitcher and quickly moved up the ranks to become a starter for the Reds in their regular rotation. If memory serves me correctly, he too threw submarines. He was the catalyst for the Reds' pennant race back in 1963. I was in the booth announcing the game against the Pirates. As I remember...."

Chapter Twenty-eight

"It's 3 and 2 against Marshall. Clemons sets up to throw... there's the pitch...Marshall slams the ball. It's a shot to right. Can Pennington get to it? Pennington knocks the ball down. Clemons is on his horse to get to first base to cover...Marshall is busting it down the line. The throw from Pennington is a little off. Clemons makes a stab for it as he reaches the bag just as Marshall gets there and 'Oh my god!' What a collision! Clemons goes rolling...Marshall is down too. It looked like Marshall did nothing to avoid the collision and Clemons never saw it coming."

"Clemons is not getting up. After a shot like that, I'm not surprised," as the announcer continued.

Chapter Twenty-nine

"...what a horrible collision covering a play at first base with another player left Clemons with torn ligaments in his throwing shoulder. That ended Clemons' pitching career and the Reds' run at the pennant that year. The Reds slid from a comfortable first place in August to finish up 3rd in the National League race," the announcer explained.

"Lucky for Clemons, the Reds saw more than just pitching potential in him and offered to keep him on as a coach in their farm system. He worked several years in the farm system as a pitching coach and later as manager for their double A farm team. I believe he even helped Ted Abernathy develop some of his pitches when Ted was with Reds. He's been the pitching coach on this level now for 11 years and he brings a wealth of knowledge with him any time he walks out to the mound."

"Strange that coach Clemons does not have anyone warming up in the bull pen. That either says that he has a lot of confidence in Morgan or, more likely, there is no one else left from the Reds' pitching staff to come in and take over at this point. This is absolutely it and they will live or die by Morgan's submarine."

In the stands Dan sat intensely silent, as did his wife. Knowing her husband like she did, she was almost afraid to say anything.

"Keep the faith, Dan, he's the one..........you're almost there."

Again the voice. He looked at his wife and realized, as usual, he alone heard it.

The pitching coach made his way to the center of the infield to meet Tanner waiting there for him.

"Ya know, a good friend once told me that life is sometimes like hitchhiking in a high plains hailstorm. You can't run, you can't hide, and you can't make it go away. You can only stand there and take it."

"But no matter how dark it gets, no matter how hard the rain comes down, no matter how close the lightning strikes, sooner or later, it begins to let up; the clouds begin to break up, and the sun begins to shine again."

"Today, you are the sun and this is your time to shine."

"Now, I know for a fact you've been taught everything you need to know. What is it that you seem to have forgotten?"

Chapter Thirty

It's the bottom of the 5th, eleven year-old Tanner was on the mound pitching. His team was losing and Tanner was struggling to keep the other team from hitting the ball. More times than not, Tanner was matched against the best teams in the league. It didn't help when he was surrounded by mostly weak teammates that were lucky to make any play without an error. He was the best pitcher on the team and one of the best in the league but he had one of the worst records.

The inning was over and Tanner walked to the dugout. By the side of the dugout, just outside the fence, was his dad and he wanted to talk. He looked exasperated.

Tanner had been working with his dad on a curveball but like everything new, it took practice and since he couldn't throw a strike with it every time, he just didn't want to throw it in a game.

"Tanner, you can't just keep throwing the same pitch over and over and think they are not going to hit it. You've got to start throwing your curveball. It's a slower speed and breaks nicely. You've got to start throwing some of those even if you don't throw a strike every time. It doesn't matter. Just throwing a different speed or a different pitch like your breaking ball keeps the batter off balance. They don't have to be all strikes."

"But Dad…"

"Just do it!!!"

With that last remark his dad turned and headed back to the bleachers to sit with his wife.

Chapter Thirty-one

"I think I need to mix my pitches up a little better. Maybe use that rising fastball some, too," said Tanner.

"Well looks like this trip to the mound was worthwhile after all. Plus it helped me get a little more TV exposure, you know, for my grandkids watching. I want them to be proud of me you know, for helping you win the game," Clemons added.

Ever since Tanner arrived in Cincy, Coach Clemons always seemed to have a way of taking the edge off of any situation.

"Seems as if Coach Clemons was taking a little too much time out at the mound for the home plate umpire and now he's heading to the mound," noticed the announcer.

"No problem here is there, Clemons?" grouched the umpire.

"No, no problem at all. Tanner's just helping me look a little more important than I really am, aren't you, son?" With that remark both coach Clemons and the umpire laughed to themselves, as if sharing an inside joke.

With a chuckle, Clemons turned and headed back to the dugout and the umpire back to home plate, leaving Tanner alone with his catcher at the mound.

"Well, you heard him, looks like a good time to use your rising fastball, and you know how you're always messing around with me with your knuckleball. Maybe you can use that pitch to mess around with them a little bit."

Tanner went full count on the next two batters using all of his pitches, but the last pitch to both batters was the rising fastball. A swing and a miss both times and he was out of the inning.

"And after six complete innings, the game is still scoreless," updated the announcer.

Top of the seventh and it was time for the seventh inning stretch. Thomas decided this was his best opportunity to hit the restroom without missing any of the game. Thomas asked his son if he needed to go to which his son responded, "No."

Once the father was gone, Dan asked what the monster book was that he had with him.

"Oh, that's my baseball card collection. I've got the cards of the best of the best baseball players that ever were."

"Really, do you mind if I have a look?"

"Sure, go ahead."

Well, now Dan had his chance to flip to page 53 and see what was so interesting on that page. Dan scanned down the page. Many names were familiar but then he got to one…Dan Morgan – Pitcher. It looked very much, well, exactly like Dan did twenty-five years ago. Dan had never been aware of any major league player with whom he shared the same name. Curious, Dan pulled the card out of its protective sleeve to read the stats on the back of the card. Strangely, there were no stats on the back. It only said he played with the Reds but gave no dates.

Dan asked Jimmy where he got this card. Jimmy said he traded for this card at the Little League ballpark where he played. Jimmy explained the umpire there had a collection of baseball cards. The umpire promised that the guy on that card was the greatest submarine pitcher that ever was.

"My dad wasn't real happy about my trade; he said he had never heard of this guy."

The kid got real quiet while Dan studied the card, then finally the kid asked, "Is that you?"

Dan stared at the card, and if he could just forget the last twenty-five years, he could almost believe that that was really him.

"No," Dan finally said, "that couldn't be me."

"Here we are in the bottom of the 7th," the announcer continued, "The count is one and two on Hernandez as he digs in. There's the wind-up, the pitch, and a big swing. Hernandez gets all of that one…it's going, going. Tommy White is not even bothering to head for the fence on that one!!! Gone!!! That one is in the upper deck…home run!!! Reds take a 1-0 lead!!!!"

The 8th inning was a continuation of the war between the Reds and the Yankees…pitching vs. hitting vs. great defensive plays. Neither side yielded to the other, and neither side scored.

"Top of the 9th inning and we'll have White, Holmes and Farmer to face off with Morgan. The Reds have been holding on precariously to the 1-0 lead since the 7th inning. Looks like Morgan is going to have to face Rocky Farmer one more time. Morgan has dodged a bullet three times against this man as he …" continued the announcer.

Morgan threw only a few warm-up pitches, no doubt conserving what energy he still had left. The long game, the long day, had left him running on reserves. The catcher took it down to the 2nd baseman who flipped the ball to the shortstop. The shortstop walked the ball over to Morgan.

"Three outs, Tanner. Give it all you've got," said the shortstop as he handed the ball over to Morgan.

The first batter, White, walks. Four straight pitches all outside the strike zone. The tension in the stadium has turned up five fold.

Standing in the immensity of the stadium, with almost 43,000 people on their feet, Tanner's world was compressed into a 60-foot area between the pitching rubber and home plate. None of the sights or sounds could enter this world, his world, only the silence, only the stillness.

"Morgan seems to be struggling now, with the leadoff batter taking a walk. Now Morgan has one man on base, nobody out, and the heavies of the Yankees' lineup waiting for their turn at the plate. Tanner's got to try to keep it together for these last three outs," said the announcer.

The second batter came up to the plate, no doubt more confident after the first walk, that Morgan was indeed struggling. He was hoping he could be the one to push the Yankee rally button and unleash the Yankee rally monkey on the Reds.

Tanner's mind was silent. He could not hear the chatter from his teammates, nor the taunts of the opposing team...nor the clamor of the crowd...only the silence...and a voice....

"Tanner...Remember the rules...the Commandments......Get ahead of the batter."

Suddenly, Tanner stepped back off the rubber and picked up the rosin bag. He thought to himself, "Where did that come from? Was that me? Were those my thoughts?"

It almost seemed like those words came from outside of his self. "The Commandments, yes, the Commandments, the ones that brought you here," he thought to himself.

Stepping back to the rubber, he took the signal from Hernandez and went into his stretch. The windup, the pitch. Hard and fast and straight...right down the middle.

"Strike one!" yelled the umpire.

"The Commandments" Tanner thought to himself, over and over again in his mind. "The Commandments"...it was like a mantra.

Like a man on a mission, Tanner took the throw from Hernandez and without hesitation he was back on the rubber, ready to take the signal from his catcher. Tanner shook off the first sign, and then nodded yes to the next, a hard slider that caught the corner and the batter looking.

"Strike two!" yelled the umpire.

Tanner quickly took the throw back from the catcher and set up for his next pitch. Tanner's pace caused the batter to back out of the box. The batter, with two strikes so quickly on him, needed to break Tanner's rhythm. Tanner didn't back off the rubber. He wasn't giving an inch and he wasn't backing down. A mental war was being waged between the pitcher and the batter and neither wanted to be the first to blink.

Finally, the umpire yelled, "Play Ball!!!" and the batter stepped back into the box.

Tanner went into his stretch, checked the runner on first and delivered his next pitch, a floating, off speed pitch. The batter tried to check his swing.

"Strike Three!!!" yelled the umpire as the batter motioned to appeal the call to the first base umpire. With some hesitation, the first base umpire motioned…"Out!!!" The call drew some wild reactions from the stands as the Yankee fans in attendance had thought he checked his swing in time.

"Looks like the umpire may have given Morgan a break on that last call. I would have to see the replay again but I thought he checked his swing and the count should be 1 and 2," noted the announcer.

"One out, one man on first and the one man that can jeopardize the one run lead held by Cincinnati is now coming to the plate."

"Rocky Farmer has led the American League in batting with an amazing .392 during the season and a Series leading .433; simply amazing! Although Farmer has been ineffective thus far today, it would seem that that would just make it all the more likely that he gets a hit as he faces a very tired Tanner Morgan. Farmer is overdue."

Tanner was quickly back on the rubber as he waited to face-off against Rocky Farmer. Farmer took his time, letting the rookie pitcher wait on him.

Finally, Farmer was finished with all of his pre-batting ritual and settled into the batter's box. Just as quickly Morgan backed off the rubber. Now it was Farmer's turn to wait on the rookie. Morgan picked up the rosin as if to give justification to his stepping off the rubber. In his mind, the mantra continued…"The Commandments"… "The Commandments"….

"Morgan no doubt realizes he will not be given any free pitches as Farmer is a great first pitch hitter. When Farmer comes to the plate, it's for one purpose…to hit the ball and he does that better than anyone in the League."

Finally the umpire yelled, "Play Ball!!!" and they were back to a face-off. Suddenly, Hernandez called timeout and went to the mound.

Hernandez held his catcher's mitt up over his mouth to hide the conversation from anyone who may read lips and said, "Tanner, it just hit me. Farmer seems to be anxious to hit the ball, he's just salivating to be the hero. Make him chase your pitch. Throw your slider low and break it outside the strike zone, see if he will chase it. I'm betting he will."

Tanner nodded affirmatively to him and Hernandez jogged back to the plate. Farmer never left the batter's box. He continued to play the mind game…not giving an inch…not backing down a step.

Upon arriving at the plate, the umpire smiled at Hernandez. Hernandez wondered why the umpire was smiling, then he thought he heard the umpire say "good plan". But with all of the noise in the stadium, Hernandez couldn't say for sure.

Morgan was ready. He checked the runner one last time and made his pitch…a hard, low slider on the outside corner. An anxious Farmer went after the pitch and ripped it down the first base side. The first baseman, Ward, made a diving stab at the ball to his right and knocked it down. Morgan was on his way to first base as Ward bounced up to recover the ball. Farmer was streaking down the first base line as Ward went to 2nd base with his throw and got the runner, the throw back to first with Morgan covering.

"Oooout!!!" yelled the first base umpire. Double play and the Reds cinch the Series.

Morgan's teammates rushed from the dugout to the infield where the on-field players had already started piling on each other in celebration. Everyone was dancing, jumping, yelling and screaming. Security was scrambling to keep thousands of fans from pouring onto the field.

"Looks like they made it! Tanner's got to be so excited!" Dan's wife commented.

"Yeah, for once he really does seem to be letting it all out. I don't know that I have ever seen him like that. Maybe he realizes that he really has made it."

Dan was on his feet along with everyone else, standing quietly, proudly, a tear in his eye, a smile on his face, unable to speak, as his son had just lived Dan's dream right before his eyes, all the way to the big dance, and came away a winner…and a hero. Dan felt as proud as if it had been him that just pitched the ballgame. That one solitary moment had made a life time of struggles, hardships, doubt and confusion all worthwhile.

Not until after what seemed like a half an hour, did the excitement and hysteria begin to fade. The Reds had left the field for the locker room to continue the celebration with dozens of media personnel in front of millions of viewers who hoped they just saw a revival of the Big Red Machine.

"Well, I guess we should think about leaving."

"Yeah, I think you're right."

"Still seems like an awful lot of people still here. It doesn't seem like anyone has actually left."

Keith or Kevin (or whatever his name was), the attendant for the VIP seats that Tanner provided came up and offered his congratulations.

"Is there anything else I can do for you folks?"

Kathleen began to say "No" but was interrupted by Dan.

"Keith, security seems to have things well in hand. Do you think I could walk out on the field, just for a minute, just to see what it's like?"

The attendant paused; a look of concern crossed his face. He knew he didn't have the authority to grant such a request, but he said, "Wait a minute." Keith purposefully headed down to the infield railing by the home team dugout where a security guard was standing, talking to someone just out of sight in the Cincy dugout.

Dan watched Keith speak to the security guard who looked at him and Kathleen then turned to the person out of sight in the dugout. Satisfied that the request seemed genuine and harmless, the guard nodded to Keith. Keith waved for Dan and Kathleen to come down to the field. The guard continued to talk to the unseen person in the dugout.

As excited as he had been at any point in the game, Dan stepped down to the dugout railing with Kathleen. Dan climbed over the railing and helped Kathleen do the same.

"Thanks, Keith, I really appreciate this."

"No problem, Mr. Morgan. Glad I could help."

Dan proceeded to walk out onto the infield grass, pausing to gaze up at the immensity of the stadium surrounding him. Surprisingly, the fans were still lingering in the stands, still in awe of the game they had just witnessed. Strolling out to the mound, Dan stepped onto the rubber. Home plate never looked so far away.

In the locker room, the chaotic celebration continued. The TV network had set up a makeshift studio in the locker room. A bank of monitors on one wall and the announcers, who were soaked with champagne as was every player on the team, went from player to player soliciting their take on the game. Tanner was no exception. He was covered inside and out with the bubbly brew.

The bank of monitors were still broadcasting from the multitude of cameras stationed throughout the stadium which had been positioned to catch every play from every perspective. Tanner saw his pitching coach over near the monitors, paying particular attention to one of them. The pitching coach turned and looked at Tanner and smiled. Then he turned back to the monitor. Tanner's curiosity drew him over to the same monitor. He saw that particular monitor was from the camera covering the pitcher's mound.

"Recognize him, Tanner?" asked the pitching coach.

Tanner saw a familiar figure standing there where he had just battled for the last three hours. Almost in disbelief, he saw his dad standing on the rubber, looking to home plate. Suddenly the world around Tanner disappeared. He didn't seem to see or hear the joyous raucous of his teammates still going on. It was as if the world and time itself had suddenly come to a stop. Another moment passes, and then Tanner looked to his locker, grabbed a ball, his glove, his spare glove and spare jersey. Without another word to anyone he quickly hustled out of the locker room. Outside the locker room were a number of fans who rushed up to congratulate him. Tanner quickly passed by them with only cursory acknowledgement. Down the breezeway he ran to the Cincinnati Reds home team dugout.

In the dugout Tanner saw the home plate umpire surprisingly still there talking to a security guard and looking out at the man occupying the pitcher's mound. Tanner's mom stood there just outside the dugout and saw Tanner. She saw the ball, the gloves, the jersey, and smiled.

Tanner walked out towards the mound.

"Hey, you look naked out there without these," as he handed his dad his glove, ball and jersey.

Dan took the jersey and saw "Morgan" across the back.

"Imagine that," he said jokingly. "Looks like they knew I was coming."

"Need a few to warm up with?"

"Yeah, just a few, well maybe more than a few, it's been a long time."

"Well, let's start easy."

Tanner and his dad tossed the ball back and forth as Tanner slowly backed up towards home plate. The cob webs in Dan's shoulder grudgingly gave way little by little with each throw. The joints groaned and creaked but submitted to Dan's efforts. It seemed that with each pitch, Dan threw off year after year of wear and tear.

Back in the home team locker room the broadcaster was looking for Tanner, the winning pitcher, for some comments on his efforts as the new kid on the block with the "Weight of the World" Series on his shoulders. His teammates also noticed his absence until their eyes were drawn to one particular TV monitor on the wall.

"What's Tanner doing out there?"

"That must be his dad; he's throwing just like Tanner."

A strange quietness fell on the locker room as everyone's attention was drawn to the monitors. They stood mesmerized at the TV screen. Other monitors showed that few if any fans had left the stands. The stadium seemed still full as they watched this oddity before them on the field.

Hernandez was first, then another player, then another, then another. They grabbed their gloves and headed out of the locker room. The broadcaster was left with a locker room devoid of players and had no choice but to follow.

On the field Tanner had squatted down behind the plate as a catcher. Dan was amazed that he was still capable of throwing the ball, and strikes to boot. He felt so alive…like he was twenty years old again.

Tanner's teammates, some with shirts pulled out loose, some shoes still un-tied, came up through the home team dugout and onto the field. The fans stood and cheered as if the players were coming back to bow to the crowd, for one more ovation, but instead, some players took their positions and a couple of players grabbed a bat and started taking some warm-up swings. Tanner's catcher, Hernandez, came over to Tanner, in full gear, suited back up to catch.

"Tanner, why don't you let me do that?" indicating that he's the catcher, not Tanner.

Excited by the prospect of playing some baseball here and now with the winners of the World Series, Dan continued to warm up when he heard someone yell from the other dugout.

"Hey, we want a rematch, double or nothing."

Apparently, all of the commotion did not go un-noticed by the Yankee players. Everyone looked over and saw several of the Yankee players coming out of their dugout.

"Sure, bring it on! We've got another barrel of Whoop Ass still to open up," Hernandez said good-naturedly.

Up in the stands, Thomas and his son, Jimmy, were still there. "See, Dad, I told you it was him," said Jimmy to his dad.

"Perhaps you were right, son. Are you up for watching another ballgame? Maybe we can hang around afterward and get that baseball card you have autographed."

"A promise made is a promise kept"

That voice, Dan knew that voice! Now he remembered that voice! But where did it come from? Dan spun around looking and his attention was drawn to the Reds dugout. There was the home plate umpire, the Man-in-Blue, previously appearing disinterested in the dugout, now he was walking out to the mound.

"I see you made it to the big dance after all. I hope you don't mind me saying I told you so."

"It was you…you all along!"

"Yes…Yes, it was Me, it has always been Me."

"I don't understand. Who are you?"

"You should know who I Am. I am the One who looked into a little boy's heart long ago and saw the will and desire of that little boy's dream that I could not say 'No' to. And I made a promise to him. But as you have seen, life doesn't always work out as planned; just a step or two off the path and you can become lost. And once lost, the journey to your destination can be much more difficult. You are basically blazing a new path where there was none…and that can be a challenge. That made the promise a little more difficult for Me to keep. I needed help, so I sent you a son. He's the one that made it possible, the one who helped Me help you. But enough of that."

"Why don't you let Me get back behind the plate and do My job?"

With that, the Man-in-Blue stepped behind the catcher, pulled His mask down over His face and yelled "Play ball!!!"

With those words, it all started to make sense. The scattered, misplaced pieces of his life started to come together into a beautiful mosaic tapestry. His soul was a story, his life was an adventure. There was meaning behind all the madness of his life after all. He finally understood, and he could finally see, and he was filled with great joy!

"Com'on Pops, show'em what you've got."

"Strike one!" cried the Man-in-Blue.

And the crowd stood and cheered.........................

Epilogue

"Wake up, Dear; it's almost 7:00.

Consciousness came on slowly as I became aware of who and where I was. The clock radio was playing some Top 40 song I had heard a hundred times. The amount of light in the room indicated that dawn was here along with the arrival of another workday.

"Uh-huh, I'm awake now."

"Sorry to have to wake you. I saw you were tossing and turning most of the night, but then you looked so peaceful this morning, I wanted to let you sleep so bad."

"Me, too, I was having a great dream, and now I can't seem to remember it, as always."

"I'm sorry, Dear, I wish I could help."

Slowly, my body started responding. I sat up on the edge of the bed, thinking of what laid before me today besides work.

"Remember Tanner and his son, Jake, have a ball game tonight. Tanner said he would probably have Jake pitching. He is really impressed with how well little Jake has picked up on the game. Allen and his wife will probably be there as well so you don't want to work late".

"That's right," I thought. I'm glad to see them and the grandkids any chance I get and the ball games make it easier to do just that. Strange, it now seems that the baseball torch has been passed to Tanner. The former player is now the coach, such as it is in lives of everyday people.

I make my way to the bathroom for my morning ritual of shaving my sparse beard in front of the mirror and see the yellowed piece of paper I had taped to the mirror a long time ago; words that I had written at another time of my life when trying to reconcile the existence of god in a godless world. Words that I thought I had once heard, just below the threshold of my consciousness.

Danny's Psalm

Blessed is he, though he has no faith, yet lives righteously.
For I will travel with him through all the days of his life.
Though he has not eyes to see My light,
Nor ears to hear My voice,
Nor feelings to know My love for him,
I will quietly, patiently, abide in his heart and wait.

Temptation may cause him to dally, but not for long.
Rocks may cause him to stumble, but not to quit.
Others may be led and led astray,
But he will find his own way,
He will decide his own fate,
While I can only watch.

Though his life is spent wandering in the deep of the forest,
He is never truly lost.
He need only turn his eyes to the heavens.
He need only turn to his heart within.
I am there, both within and without.

His joys are My joys.
His trials are My trials.
His pain, is My pain. .
The things that he stands for, fights for, and lives for,
Are the things that I Am.

His path may take him through the Valley of the Shadow of Death,
Through the Dark Night of his Soul,
Or to the very mountaintop where he believes Me to be.
He may find Me anywhere, for wherever he is,
I Am and Will Always Be.

I long for the day when he will awaken from his dream.

The Man-in-Blue

The End

Author's Comments:

Well, if you made it this far, you must have thought it was worth finishing. I hoped you enjoyed it and thought it was a good read. I do suggest that you take the time to read it again. I think you would pick up on things that you may have missed the first time through that would make it worth reading one more time.

But the story doesn't necessarily end here. I may write the 'second verse' to Danny's Song, we'll see.

If you enjoyed the story, please recommend my book to your friends on Facebook or elsewhere and drop me an e-mail at dannyssong_thebook@yahoo.com. I am probably biased, but I think this story would make a great movie, so if you know any movie producers, lol.

If you are interested in how this story came to be, it started with me day dreaming while lying in bed on a Sunday morning, letting my mind just wander when I dreamed up what was to be the ending of this story. Well, no, that's not exactly right. If I go back to the very beginning, when the story really began, I go back to the time I was a little boy dreaming of playing for the Reds, but if you read the story, you probably already figured that out. The story was some personal meaning for me and I tried to tell it as good as I could. This endeavor to write a story worth reading became the one item on my "bucket list" that I would have always regretted if I did not finish and publish it. Now I can cross the one and only "have-to-do" item off of my "bucket list".